THE SALESMAN

Dick Totino

Printed in the United States of America

First Printing March 2018

ISBN 978-1-945604-16-4 Paperback

ISBN 978-1-64255-415-1 e-Book

Published by: Book Services
                www.BookServices.us

Contents

Chapter One 1
Chapter Two 9
Chapter Three 19
Chapter Four 31
Chapter Five 39
Chapter Six 55
Chapter Seven 62
Chapter Eight 73
Chapter Nine 88
Chapter Ten 95
Chapter Eleven 105
Chapter Twelve 114
Chapter Thirteen 123
Chapter Fourteen 138
Chapter Fifteen 145
Chapter Sixteen 154
Chapter Seventeen 169
Chapter Eighteen 183
Chapter Nineteen 195
Chapter Twenty 213
Chapter Twenty-One 219
Chapter Twenty-Two 227
Chapter Twenty-Three 235
Chapter Twenty-Four 243
Chapter Twenty-Five 249
Chapter Twenty-Six 260
Chapter Twenty-Seven 264

About the Author 267

The Salesman

Chapter One

Bzzz

Bzzz

Bzzz

"Shit!"

It was morning already. As Yogi might say, 'morning comes early around here.' Too damned early this morning.

His right hand materialized from under the warm covers, its fingers skittering along the surface of the bedside table, searching for the source of the annoying vibrations, a little black plastic unit that was almost invisible in the dark. He finally felt it under his fingers and managed to press the correct button on his cell phone.

The only light in the room had to sneak in around the shabby vinyl slats covering the distant window. The yellow glow told him that it was still dark outside. The light was coming from the security poles whose fixtures illuminated the parking lot in front of the moderately-priced room he currently occupied.

His left arm was numb, the weight of her head cutting off the circulation to his hand. Her long sweet-smelling blonde hair covered her face and flowed over his arm and neck. She didn't move when the alarm vibrated. She slept soundly, exhausted from their nearly nightlong love making.

"Hey!" he whispered in her ear, trying to gently wake her. "Hey, Baby, time to wake up."

She moaned and rolled away from him just far enough to allow the blood to rush down his arm. He could feel the cold tingling and stinging of the flow as it reached his fingers.

He slid gently out of bed and walked into the bathroom. He showered and shaved and dressed in his usual uniform of the day: conservative dark suit, white button-down collar shirt, featureless tie. As he reentered the bedroom, she awoke and watched as he packed the last of his clothes into his leather carry-on and stuff a stack of papers into his briefcase.

He looked down at her. She was stunning. A classic beauty. She sat up and leaned back against the false head-board that was miraculously affixed to the wall beneath a framed picture of an enormous gaudily-colored flower that could not possibly exist anywhere on earth except in the warped mind of a Walmart merchandise buyer. It too was bolted to the wall, should anyone entertain the idea of stealing it to upgrade their home decor.

The bed sheet fell away, exposing firm breasts that needed no support. She was not in the least embarrassed by her nakedness. And, oh yes dear God, she was beautiful. Five feet four, maybe five. Luminous hazel eyes that shone even in the piss-poor light washing over her. Soft lips. Mid-twenties at most. If only he could remember her name!

He stepped toward the bed and sat down next to her. Her face lit up with a smile as he reached out and stroked her hair, running his hand down over her shoulder and continuing across the silky-smooth skin of her breasts.

"I've gotta go," he said. "Got to catch a plane."

She smiled again, one hand holding his firmly against her body, the other lacing itself around his neck. She was so soft and smelled so sweet. It would be so easy to toss his briefcase aside and slip back into bed with her, to just get lost for the rest of the day having sex repeatedly until neither of them could walk. But, he couldn't.

He tried to stand. She leaned her face into his, pulling him closer and kissing him softly. She was ever so tempting. Why was she here? Why does such a beautiful young woman lower herself to being picked up in a bar and give up her dignity to a man she had never met? Spend a night filled with nothing more than physical sex. Did she think that anything would come from it? A permanent relationship? Love? Real love?

It made him question the way that those of her generation valued themselves. Was it so easy to give up your body to nothing more than a night's worth of empty pleasure? To lie naked with a man you had known for only an hour or two in a sleazy bar?

"When will you be back in town?" she asked.

"I'm not sure. Two weeks," he lied. "Maybe three."

"Will you call me?"

"Of course. I'd like that," he lied again with a practiced tone and reassuring gentleness. All the while knowing damn well that he would not, *could* not, ever see her again. "Why don't you write your phone number down for me while I finish getting my stuff together, and I'll call you a few days before I come back? We'll get together then."

He was hoping that she would include her name so he could say a proper goodbye. As much for his own sake as for hers, he didn't want to treat her as trash. However, they often didn't have a first name. Or any name. The women in his life rarely ever had a last. And almost never an address. Just a number. Just ten digits of identity that would be torn up moments after his leaving.

Of course, she didn't know that there was a deeper motive than just sex for her being in his bed. The night with her was far more pleasurable than expected, but less than twenty-four hours earlier, he was carrying out an assignment. A mission assigned to him by the government agency he worked for.

He was a man with two lives. The first, a public life as a well-established chemical salesman jumping from country to country negotiating deals with huge international companies, as well as with governments.

The second, using the first as a cover, an assassin secretly employed by a covert government agency whose task it was to secretly and silently remove anyone who stood in the way of the interests of the United States of America.

The name he was most often known by was John N. Anderson, although he used many other names during his travels. He was equally good and highly rewarded in each of his two lives.

The day before encountering the young woman currently warming his bed, he was approaching a sprawling three-story home tucked into a semi-private cove on Lake Norman, just to the north and west of Charlotte, North

Carolina. He chose the lake approach to minimize the risk of being seen. Dressed in the proper fashion of an avid paddler, he looked like any other sportsman out for a day on the water.

But he wasn't. He was here for an entirely different purpose. The boat dock he was about to tie up to was owned by the vice president of the international banking department of a very large bank headquartered in Charlotte.

The vice president had been under government scrutiny for almost two years. It was known that he was manipulating accounts to illegally funnel huge amounts of money to terrorist groups in the Middle East. In the process, he too was getting very rich. But he was slick, and the government couldn't quite get the proof needed to arrest him and bring him to trial. The money he transferred illegally was costing American lives.

Since the route to the courtroom was barred by his skills as a crook, he could not be brought to justice in the most desired way. But there were those in Washington who believed a demonstration of violence very often served to deliver a different and more effective kind of message—one that the terrorists understood more than they did the rule of law.

That's where John came in. He was the deliverer of the message...and the violence. Fast. Ruthless. Relentless. Final. That was his stock in trade, and it was his success over the years that had made him a rich man. Killing wasn't cheap.

He tied the kayak to the dock and slowly ambled up the sloping lawn toward the house. He didn't try to conceal himself. Instead, should anyone be watching him, he acted as if he were looking for assistance of some sort. His plan worked.

When he was little more than a few of paces from the elevated deck at the rear of the house, a man in his mid-fifties stepped out and called to him.

"This is private property. What can I do for you?"

"Oh, hey," John replied, using a southern greeting. "I broke my paddle and need to find another. I might have to get to the nearest marina to buy one. Can you tell me where the closest place is?"

The man paused for a moment. "I might be able to help you. I think I have a couple of extra paddles. Walk around that end of the house, and I'll meet you at the front of the garage. See what we can do."

"Thank you so much," John replied.

He knew the banker would be home alone. He had studied the household habits for over a month and knew that his wife always spent Saturday afternoons with her mother in Statesville, about forty miles from Charlotte. She wouldn't be returning home for at least three or four hours.

He walked around the corner of the house as the garage door was pulling itself up. The owner greeted him by extending his hand and introducing himself to John. John returned the greeting using a name that just happened to pop into his head.

"Wait here. I'll see what I can find for you. They should be in the storage closet back toward the rear."

"Thanks," John replied as he moved toward the control for the garage door. Using his elbow to avoid leaving any fingerprints, he pressed the control to lower the door. In a heartbeat he was behind the vice president, withdrawing a .22 caliber pistol from under his shirt. He placed the muzzle at the base of the man's skull and pulled the trigger twice.

The double tap would ensure that the killing would appear to be a professional job. That would make the message being sent very clear to those on the receiving end of the dirty money. The man fell to the floor, not even knowing that he was dead. The two small slugs circling around inside of his skull would turn his brain into tapioca pudding in seconds.

John calmly turned and walked toward the single doorway at the side of the garage, exiting onto the side yard without looking back. He didn't have to. He knew exactly what the effects were on the man. He had done this far too many times to doubt the results.

He slowly walked back down to the dock, climbed into the kayak, and paddled himself back across the lake. When he reached the spot where he had parked his rental car near the town of Denver, he abandoned the kayak, leaving it to float away. He then drove himself southeast along NC Highway 16 to the room he had rented in a national chain. It was located at the intersection of Little Rock Road and I-85. He chose this area because of its proximity to the airport.

Secondly, the hotel had a very active lounge, and since it was Saturday, he knew there would be a good crowd that night for him to blend into. Luckily, he found the young woman with whom he had just spent a very rewarding night. Unknowingly, she was part of his potential alibi. A part of his plan.

He also made sure his face would appear on the security cameras in the hotel lobby. In the highly unlikely event that someone had seen him at the Lake Norman house, he wanted to be sure he could create and support a claim that he was right here in his hotel the entire time. But, he knew he wouldn't be recognized. He was far too good at what he did and the way that he did it. However, caution was a part of his overall plan. Covering his tracks worked, and everyone knew you couldn't be in two places at the same time.

The young lady with the fantastic perky breasts would also serve him well. If need be to protect her good name, she would swear to her long dead great-grandmother that she was in love with him and would do anything for him… including lying. But it was time to leave her to become a part of his history. His secret history.

Chapter Two

Within a few minutes of their final kiss, he was in his rental car headed toward the airport with 'Jackie 555-555-0100' in his pocket and the sweet taste of her on his lips. The goodbye went well, done with grace and tenderness and at least as much dignity as could be expected after a one-nighter. He felt certain, fortified by her moist eyes, that it was her first. Her first experience being left alone in a cheap motel room after giving yourself completely to your "date." Unfortunately, it wasn't his.

But right now he had other things to be concerned with. He had to make a phone call. He entered the airport causeway and looked for the signs directing him to the rental car return area. Once the turn-in process was completed, he rode to the terminal in the shuttle and walked up to the ticket counter to get his seat assignment. He would carry on his only travel bag.

Traveling through airports assisted his invisibility. Unless a person acted like an ass, arguing with an airline employee about a thirty-minute flight delay caused by

The Salesman

a thunderstorm fifteen hundred miles away that she had absolutely no control over, no one saw anyone in an airport. No one looked you in the eye. No one saw you walk by unless your boobs or your ass were hanging out, and then all they saw was the boobs or the ass. Airports were impersonal deserts filled with people concerned with no one other than themselves. Great places to hide.

After clearing security, he walked toward the gate assigned to his flight. As he approached, he saw a group of telephones mounted to the wall across from a newsstand. Fast disappearing in favor of cell phones, these fading old-fashioned public telephones were where he usually made his mandated weekly call.

For lack of attention, the signal from one of these relics would be lost in the ether encompassing the world, unlike a cell phone. He and his call would remain anonymous.

Anonymous! He had always been anonymous, from the time he was a little boy growing up on an apple farm near a tiny town in the Hudson Valley of New York. Always alone. Always the "little guy," at least until he entered his senior year in high school when he had a growth spurt and shot up to six foot three inches and topped two hundred and twenty pounds.

It was then that he was shown a new level of attention and respect from his fellow male classmates. But by then it was too late. By then he enjoyed being anonymous. He had learned how to be alone and to enjoy his time living in the shadows. The pain from years of rejection was behind him, and it was his time to turn away from those who now hungered for his attention and friendship.

Chapter Two

The football and basketball coaches both tried to talk him into playing. In his own way, he told them to shove it "where the sun doesn't shine." Same with the girls. Those in his class, as well as a year or two behind, suddenly paid him a lot of attention. He used it to his advantage, enjoying their physical offerings while rejecting them in a way of payback for years of being ignored. Payback was sweet!

His father described him to others as a loner. One of the negative building blocks of their relationship. He learned, however, to accept that tag with a level of comfort that helped him enjoy being alone. Being within himself. Being at peace with who he had become. And he learned to find comfort in the natural world around him.

He grew strong physically and psychologically. To many, he became the threat instead of the threatened. The boys who had teased and demeaned him for years now tried to enter his sphere. He let them think they had, while playing them along in his new game.

Late in his senior year, his parents were killed in the crash of a single engine airplane that his father was flying. He had flown into a cloud bank, losing sight of the end of the runway and crashed two hundred yards short of a safe landing. Now John was truly alone.

He inherited the farm, as well as a sizable estate that included a seven-figure life insurance payout from a policy his father had taken out years ago. This left him independent. So, after completing his final months of high school, while living with an aunt, he engaged an attorney to liquidate all his assets and left his hometown never to look back. In his mind, it was a place where he was unwelcome and unwanted.

The Salesman

He entered the University of North Carolina at Chapel Hill, where he found a new level of acceptance. The students and staff knew nothing of his past except what he chose to tell them, and he told them very little. He majored in chemical engineering and found a fascinating new field of interest, graduating summa cum laude.

He had several girlfriends during his time in college, none of which excited him beyond the short term. There was only one woman who commanded his lasting interest. The one he was about to speak to on the telephone. The woman he knew as Kristin Blake.

He also discovered the martial arts while in college and became very proficient in several different disciplines. He found that his training helped burn off a lot of unchanneled energy when he was without a girlfriend.

After graduation he was recruited by many international chemical firms. In addition, he was approached by representatives of two or three government agencies wanting him to enlist in their activities.

However, he decided that he wanted to learn more about himself and the world. He enlisted in the military. With a college degree in his pocket, he could have become a commissioned officer. As an officer, he would be treated with a degree of importance and respect, missing in his formative years.

He chose instead to stay in the enlisted ranks. He spent three years in the U.S. Army. His service offered him the opportunity to obtain physical training that he never had in school. He volunteered for airborne training to become a paratrooper. Because of his service, he traveled to the Middle East, and found himself fighting alongside a different class of men from the selfish egotistical athletes he had known in high school. These were young men willing to earn their way in life by serving others, not by being catered to and admired because they could run fast or throw a ball fifty yards.

His combat experience also taught him about life. He was a young man suddenly confronted with the reality and fragility of life. He learned that the most impactful way to learn about life was to learn about death. Death qualified the importance of life and where he fit into it. It taught him that nothing else was anywhere near as important as life, except maybe honor.

Death taught him how to place things in priority. When one of his closest army friends was killed while standing right next to him, all else in his life fell into place. All else lost its importance. He gained a new sense of control and calm. But nothing compared to life. Death made all other matters pale in comparison and enabled him to take all other events in stride. To others, he seemed unemotional.

He wasn't. He had learned the real value of a shiny new car or the fancy clothes or expensive cell phone or the big screen TV. None compared, and if this made him unemotional, he could very easily live with that.

What he had learned was that in the grand scheme of things death, on a scale of zero to ten, ranked as one hundred and one. Most other events in life ranked somewhere less than the ten level. This would be of increasing importance in the life that lay ahead of him.

While serving in three different countries scattered across this troubled section of the globe, he came under fire numerous times. He witnessed young men, his friends, being shot and blown apart daily. One moment, his friend was either sleeping on the cot next to him or eating a meal on the other side of the table and a moment later, his body was being carted away in a black vinyl bag, bloodied and in ruin.

He also learned how to kill. It was only the first time that upset him. After that, killing got easier. He wasn't sure if it was because he was getting used to it or the more he saw his fellow soldiers blown apart, the more it became justified. Either way, he learned and he learned well, surviving when others perished.

As time passed and he experienced more death, he became detached, feeling less and less for each person he saw die, as well as for those he killed.

Despite all of this, he enjoyed the entire experience of the military. As his enlistment time ended, he was approached to reenlist, to extend his time in uniform. He was strongly inclined to stay in the service for an additional tour of duty. However, those representing various government agencies who had tried to recruit him while he was in college renewed their efforts. They wanted him to join another kind of service. Those who had approached him from the industry side wanted him to accept a position in the chemical industry.

Ultimately, with the help and guidance of one of the agencies, he did both. After completing his military service, he joined a very large international chemical company headquartered just south of Philadelphia. He was placed in a sales training position where he was exposed to their line of products with the aim of becoming an international technical sales representative. The job would involve a lot of travel, which meant a lot of time alone. Perfect!

Chapter Two

His new job made him the ideal candidate for the agency that had recruited him. He trained and worked for the chemical giant while spending his weekends and summer vacation being trained by the agency at their secure location in northern Virginia.

Little did he know or care where this marriage of salesman and government agent would lead him. In the nearly fifteen years since he entered his dual life, he had traveled the world. While completing duties for both his employers, he became very wealthy, earning high commissions as a highly visible and respected technical sales rep, along with fees for being invisible while completing classified missions.

All this led him to where he found himself at this very moment. Picking his way through a major airport using his cover as a salesman to avoid detection as a deadly agent.

He knew how to get lost in an airport. Even with all the modern surveillance equipment, there were ways. He could disappear quickly if necessary, which was usually the case. Airports had lots of doors leading to all sorts of places. Lots of people of all shapes, sizes and colors to blend in with. Lots of alternate routes by which to escape. Lots of hiding places. And lots of killing places. Lots of shadows for him to melt into just like he did when he was a boy.

He studied airports. Not so he could write a book or some sort of travel guide. He studied them to know where to run. To know where to hide. To do his job and escape. Quickly. Silently. Invisibly. And most importantly of all—alive.

He didn't have too much to say during these weekly telephone calls. They always began pretty much the same way and had one of two endings. Either he would spend another week on the road as a salesman, or he would get a new "assignment."

"Kristin Blake, please," he said calmly.

The usual wait before her very female, very sexy voice said, "Hello."

"Kristin?" *He wasn't sure if that was her real name or not, but it was the only name he knew her by.*

"Yes?"

"It's John. John Anderson." *His operational name, for the moment at least. Except she knew who he really was.*

"Johnny, how are you?" *Johnny. Nice touch. That was new.*

"I'm fine thanks, and you?"

"Oh, I'm fine," she answered. "Are you in town, or are you headed this way anytime soon?" *The signal for him to report for a face- to-face meeting. Highly unusual.*

"As a matter of fact, I'm headed your way toward the end of the week. That's why I called. How about we get together for lunch on Friday?"

"Oh, I'm tied up on Friday. Any chance of us getting together earlier in the week?" *Urgent, come in ASAP. Now he was on full alert.*

Chapter Two

"Okay! I'd really like to see you. Let me see what I can do with my flight schedule. I'm heading into a client's office in a moment. Why don't I call you back around four this afternoon, and I'll let you know what I'm able to arrange for Wednesday?" *I'll be there by 4:00 pm today.*

"That would be great, John. If you can make it, I'll try to meet you at the airport and buy you a drink." *She was going to meet him at the airport. Again, highly unusual. Something very strange was going on. He wondered what was up.*

"Hey," he jumped in. "I've got an idea. I'm going to need a car while I'm in town, so why don't I just go ahead and meet you afterward. Do you remember that little Italian place just north of town? How about we meet there. I'll buy you dinner." *He was coming into BWI, to the north of D.C., not Reagan National or Dulles.*

"Yeah! I remember. That's a great idea. Sounds like a date. I'll meet you there. See you on Wednesday." *She would pick him up at the designated place, the Avis car rental office.*

"Okay! I'll be there unless it snows or I get tied up with someone." *Tied up with someone. He'll be arriving on United.*

"Look forward to seeing you, Johnny. 'bye."

"Goodbye," he returned and softly hung up the plastic handset. To anyone listening, two friends had just made a dinner date at an Italian restaurant somewhere just north of some town somewhere, sometime after four in the afternoon on Wednesday. The truth was far different.

The Salesman

He arrived at Baltimore-Washington International Airport shortly after noon that day. It was Sunday, not Wednesday. He retrieved his leather bag from the overhead compartment and walked off the plane. He went directly to the ground transportation area and found his way to the car-rental shuttle bus area, where he took the one marked for Avis.

He only used Avis when he was meeting with Kristin. It was a predesignated pickup point. The only standard he would allow in his routine. However, this was the first time it was ever being used. In all the years they had been working together, she had never met him or picked him up at this airport...or any other. Something very different was going on. Very strange and he didn't like it, he didn't trust strange. Not at all. Strange could get him dead!

Chapter Three

He had met her face to face only three other times. The first was when she was appointed to be his contact or control within the organization, his "handler." The second was shortly after her appointment, when they participated in a week-long field training program designed to get them acquainted with one another, sort of a trust-building exercise. And the third time, the last time, was about two years ago after he had completed a mission of unusual sensitivity and he was called in for a very detailed, very unusual, face-to-face debriefing.

He knew very little about her, only the basics. Only what was absolutely necessary. She was thirty-four years old now. Dark eyes. Dark hair. Five foot five. About one hundred fifteen pounds. Very pretty, very sexy and…very single. She was dedicated to her job. A real career girl. All business, even at the expense of any personal life. She was so all-business, she was sure to let him know exactly what her limits were by treating him with cool professionalism. She made sure that he kept his distance.

She fascinated him, intrigued him almost to the point of daydreaming over what might be. The thought of her was the one link to a different life that he hung onto. Her movie-star looks reminded him strongly of Jessica Chastain. When with her, he had to fight the urge to stare.

Only when she was taking his mandatory weekly check-in call did the "act" of a warm personal relationship exist between them. Otherwise, all business. They had never been together intimately or even socially. But he knew damn well he wouldn't pass up the chance to spend a night with her if she ever gave him the opportunity. She was at least a nine point nine on his female ranking scale of ten, and he had never met a ten.

She was only the second control officer he had worked with in his fifteen-year career. The first, Helen, had suddenly evaporated after a failed assignment that almost cost him his life. And, more importantly, exposure of his real identity. She failed and failure was not acceptable. Not permitted in their line of work. She fucked up, and she paid the price.

This week's call, signaling him to come in for a face-to-face, was very strange, extremely unusual, and very risky. He didn't like it one little bit. Meeting like this put him at risk of being exposed, and that could lead to an untimely end.

Considering all of this, he sure hoped it proved to be justified. It worried him and made him leery of the whole process. His guard was up. His senses raw. Meetings like this caused men like him to be found dead in back alleys around the world.

He deplaned and walked through the terminal to the lower level, where the car rental desks were located. He walked outside without stopping and boarded the Avis shuttle bus. Along with two other "suits," two businessmen carrying the mandatory briefcase in one hand and a single piece of luggage in the other. Invisible all. The ride provided him the opportunity to detect if anyone was following him.

When they arrived at the Avis rental lot, he allowed the other two men to disembark first. When the bus pulled away from the curb, he walked to the left of the building and got into the waiting white four-door Ford sedan that bore a magnetic sign on the front door with the name of a nationally known real estate company.

"You're clean," she said. "No one is following you."

"Well, hello to you too, Ms. Kristin. So good to see you again. Yes, I'm well; thank you for asking," he said sarcastically. "And why would anyone be following me? The question is, is anyone following you?"

"Just a precaution," she added. "And no, no one is following me either."

"Good! Now, where are we going?"

"My place."

"Oh? Well, things are looking up!"

"Forget it, Mr. Anderson. My place has desks, copy machines, and walls that hear."

"How sexy and romantic. Can't wait. Got any beer?"

She exited the airport and took the southbound ramp onto I-295, the old Baltimore-Washington Expressway, toward D.C. They drove silently for twenty minutes. She stayed in the left-hand lane the entire time. Suddenly, and without any warning to him, as they were approaching an exit ramp, she snapped the steering wheel to the right, cutting in front of an oncoming car in that lane.

Anderson grabbed onto the dash with one hand and the door grip with the other. "What the hell was that all about?"

She did not respond. Instead she ran the stop sign at the base of the ramp and turned left, causing an oncoming car to slam on its brakes. She passed under the expressway and again snapped the wheel to the left, cutting off an oncoming delivery van that slammed on its brakes to avoid a head-on collision. She continued up the southbound ramp, re-entering the expressway, but now driving south toward Baltimore.

"Like I said, what the hell was that all about? You're a wreck looking for a place to happen." As he tried to regain his seating, he saw her eyes glancing at the rearview mirrors.

"Do I really need to explain to an experienced agent such as yourself?" He knew the answer to his question before even asking it.

"Well?" she asked.

"Nope! We're good. How about giving me a little warning next time? You scared the crap out of me, cut off three vehicles within ten seconds, broke at least half a dozen traffic laws, and nobody's following us?"

"Nope!"

He sat back in his seat. "Not bad for a desk jockey. And thanks for the thrill ride. It's been a rather boring day up until now. Plus, I think you have my bowels moving, which has been a problem for me the past few days."

"You're welcome."

They continued north toward Baltimore without any further conversation. After half an hour, they reached I-95 and entered the Baltimore Harbor Tunnel. After exiting the tunnel, she continued a few miles further north until she exited onto I-695 west. Shortly after that, she turned onto I-83 north. She took exit 17 for Padonia Road in Timonium and turned west into a residential area on a hillside overlooking the interstate.

"You've moved," he said finally breaking the silence.

"Quite regularly, just as you do," she replied very matter-of-factly.

"If I'd known we were coming this far, I'd have packed a lunch," he said as she slowed, constantly checking her mirrors to see if anyone was behind her.

"No need, we won't be here long enough to eat."

She pulled into the driveway of a 1950s tri-level. There was a For Sale sign stuck in the front yard with a logo matching the one on the side of their car. No other vehicles were in sight, either in the driveway or on the street. But Anderson knew they weren't alone, and he knew they weren't at her place either. They entered through the front door, stepping into a foyer with a living room half a level up and a den half a level below.

There was no furniture. No pictures on the walls. No drapes or window dressings of any kind. A quick check of the kitchen, dining room, and bedrooms showed that the same interior decorator had put the finishing touches on the rest of the house…total eggshell from floor to ceiling.

"Nice place you have here," he said dryly.

"It'll do. Downstairs please," she said, and led the way.

"But not your place?"

"I was just teasing you," she grinned.

The downstairs den was half-buried in the hillside; small windows overlooked the front yard. There was one door in the wall across from the staircase, presumably leading out to the two-car garage. The room was decorated in the same tasteful manner as the rooms upstairs. *Talk about staging,* he thought.

"This way please." Kristin led the way down a short hallway and through a door into an unfinished basement area typical of the cookie-cutter floor plan of this 1950s home.

In the center of the room was a square folding table and four metal folding chairs. Two men in dark blue business suits occupied the two chairs farthest from the doorway. They stood when Kristin and John entered.

The shorter of the two extended his hand as a greeting. "Mr. Anderson, I believe."

"For now," John replied, gripping his hand firmly.

The man greeting him gestured for the two to take seats in the empty chairs. When all were seated, it was John Anderson who spoke first.

"Well, is someone going to fill me in? Why the who's-following-us routine in the airport? Why the stunt-car drive getting here? And why the lovely suburban retreat? And why the hell am I being dragged in for a meeting and being put at risk of being linked to you two clowns—whoever you are?"

"John," the taller man continued. "My name, at least for this meeting, is Bruce. Bruce LaBue. This gentleman is Andrew Gore. Andrew is Kristin's boss. And I'm his."

"Okay," John replied. "I'm impressed. Getting pretty high-up here, aren't we?" His sarcasm was a purposeful way of showing his contempt for these bureaucrats who sat back in the hallways of Washington playing with people's lives and letting them know that he didn't adhere to the normal "boss" company hierarchy.

"Sort of," Bruce answered, "but the ladder goes a lot higher up on this meeting."

"Okay, so what's up? Oh, and just so you know, being called in for this meeting really pisses me off no end. You put my life and everyone in this room in jeopardy, to say nothing about any future assignments I might be given. Just so you know where I'm coming from," John said, cutting to the chase.

After a short pause and seemingly ignoring John's statement, Bruce began again. "John, how much money have you made from us over the years? Ten million? Fifteen?"

"You know exactly how much. You guys write the checks and lick the stamps, or should I say the transfers of funds. What's the point? Are we here for a performance review? Am I due for a raise? Are you going to change my benefits package and add dental coverage? I could do with a couple more weeks of paid vacation. No, dental. Let's go for the dental."

"The point is," Bruce jumped in, "that this one assignment we've got, this one assignment, will pay as much as you've been paid in total up to now. The fee is twenty-five million. And…if you want, you can call it quits when it's done with."

"Hold on, hold on!" John came back at him. "That's two biggies in one mouthful. Twenty-five million and I can quit? The twenty-five mil I can deal with if the subject justifies. But since when do you guys let guys like me quit? We're not allowed to quit. We're only allowed to die; some old and gray, most young and worn out. But dying is our only pre-approved retirement package. Besides, what do I have to do for twenty-five million? Kill the president?"

There was a long, uncomfortable silence in the room. Kristin and the two strangers exchanged glances and then stared at John.

"You've got to be kidding me. You guys aren't going to try that stunt again? Not another JFK routine? I'm not Lee Harvey Oswald."

"Not ours—" Andrew blurted out.

"Not ours? You mean someone else's? Someone else's president is the target?"

"Um…yes," Andrew replied sheepishly.

"Oh! Well, then I guess it's okay. What the hell is one president more or less in this fucked up world."

It was dead quiet. John was stunned by what he had heard, but he couldn't show those emotions. His question had gotten right to the heart of the reason he had been called in for this meeting, but the answer took him totally by surprise. And looking at Kristin, he knew immediately that she was equally surprised and shocked by the pending assignment. He was sure she hadn't known what the assignment was until this very moment.

He had been a government contract agent for years. Wet work, assassinations, sanctions, whatever you wanted to label them, had been his specialty ever since he was recruited in college.

At the time, he was their favorite type of person to be recruited. Young! Patriotic to a fault! Unafraid! Indestructible! Naïve! Alone with nowhere to go. No one waiting for him. Both his parents dead and only one sister who was much older than he and whom he saw only once every couple of years. He wasn't even sure where she lived or if she even remembered his first name half of the time. And he wasn't sure she was still alive.

He was smart and quick-witted. Fast on his feet. Good looking. A commanding presence, yet able to fade into a crowd without much effort. He could dominate a group and leave without a trace. A man with nothing to lose and not afraid of losing what he had. A young man with little past personal life, less present life, and almost no future.

That was sixteen years ago when he was in his mid-twenties. For three years they took every spare moment of his time to train him to be a killer. Every vacation. Every day off from his sales duties. His body only took a few weeks to condition. He was in remarkably good shape from his martial arts training.

It was the brain that took the time to train. It was the mind that took the time to teach ruthlessness. Time to become a smooth, silent, deadly instrument that would follow orders without looking back, without regret, without concern, without asking questions. An instrument that would react without thinking.

They also helped him further his education. He earned a Masters and a PhD in chemistry so he could hide behind his cover identity as an international chemical salesman, so he could blend in with the worldwide petrochemical industry and travel the world without any other justification. That was his cover and thus his official code name: The Salesman. "Doctor Salesman," as Kristin liked to tease him.

John Anderson and all the other names were false. Fake and empty. He had dozens, created as he needed them, discarded and tossed off when he was finished with them. He doubted that even the men in the room with him right now knew his real name.

His public career gave him a reason to travel anywhere in the world he needed to go. He was known in the industry as a wheeler-dealer, a rainmaker. A high-risk taker, ready to buy and sell shiploads of chemicals, paid handsomely for his product and services. He was known to be honest and reliable, a man who delivered to both his buyers and his sellers. They did not know that he was a deadly killer hiding within his job.

In the early stages of his training, his first assignments were tests. Rough up this guy. Scare the crap out of that one. Deliver a clear threat to the next. His first sanction came near the end of his training. A minor South American diplomat whose mouth got a little too big for his own good, as well as that of some powerful others.

Next, a U.S. businessman who couriered information between New York and the Middle East. He suddenly got a bit too curious and opened an envelope that wasn't addressed to him. Being nosy in his world was a fatal disease for which there was only one cure.

There were others. All "tests" and all passed with flying colors. All conducted under close observation by those training him. If he was instructed to make it look like an accident, it did. A slippery road or a loose rug at the top of a long staircase. A sudden heart attack or a mysterious fever.

If the powers in Washington wanted a message sent via the kill, he did that equally well. A bullet finding its target in a very public place with an exploding skull spraying brain matter over dozens of bystanders. A knife delivered in a quiet neighborhood or a busy street or in a dark theater. A noisy little bomb wired to a golf cart on a fancy private country club course. He had used them all with equal efficiency and effect.

He had never missed. Never failed. His record was a string of successful missions throughout the world. And he had never been close to being caught, except once. That was the time Helen screwed up and she'd lost her job and, he believed, her life.

Now, in the second half of his thirties, he was in superb physical, emotional, and mental condition. An accomplished killer. A deadly specimen. The number one killer in the underground world of dirty diplomatic power games. If it was big, if it was important, if it had to be done cleanly, he was the man they called upon. He was Washington's last and final answer to getting its own way.

His real name? He'd almost forgotten it, lost in the years of living in the shadow world. It had been years since he'd used it in any way other than when he visited or spoke to his sister on the phone. Kristin knew what it was. Kristin knew everything.

Martin. Lucas Martin...John Anderson... and fifty others. The Salesman.

Chapter Four

He had never been ordered to kill a president before. Diplomats and politicians at this level were usually not touched by men like him. This was new territory.

"Okay," he responded quickly to hide his shock. "Who... when... where... and how?"

"Not why?" asked Andrew.

"As dumb as I might think this assignment is, I don't ask why. I never ask why. That's your business, Andy. I don't care about why. You give me the target. I do the job. You pay me. Simple.

"And if you don't pay me? You jump right to the top of my list as my new favorite pastime." He redirected his gaze from Andrew to the man called Bruce. "And up the line I go until I get paid. Easy! That's the only *why* I'm concerned with. If I don't get paid, I don't ask why. You just die. Very simple system. Very efficient. And so far, very effective.

"So, let's start with who," John said.

Bruce and Andrew stiffened in their seats. John's little speech shifted control of this meeting back into his hands very quickly. The two men knew that they had just been warned by the best in the business. That's why he was here, and that's why they had ordered him in from his world of smoke, the world he existed in. And he had just delivered a frightening message that both men knew he could and would carry out to the letter.

"Are you threatening us?" Bruce finally managed to squeeze past the very tiny hole left in his desert-dry throat, his face flushed red with both anger and fear.

"Not at all, Bruce. Not me! Not on your life… so to speak. I don't threaten. I deliver. You guys are in the threatening business. Me? I just do a job. I'm the guy who backs up your threats. I put the muscle into your words. And I get paid well for that. But you already know that, don't you, Bruce. You know exactly what I get paid. And now you know what happens if I don't."

The room felt as if it were encased in cement. The tension and silence stiffened everyone. Bruce and John stared into each other's eyes. The message had been delivered. Now they both understood that this was a deadly serious game they were playing and it was clear who made the rules.

"Gentlemen," Andrew broke in, attempting to defuse the tension. "There's no need for doubt here. We have a lot to discuss. How about we move on. We've all got our own job to do." His voice had a noticeable quiver as he continued. "Bruce, why don't you sit down and explain to Mr. Anderson what we need? Have a seat John, please.

Please, let's all take a seat. We've got lots of work to do. We have a lot to talk about. Okay! John, are you ready?"

"Always," the agent responded, never unlocking his piercing gaze from the man across the room. The test of wills in this game was being set. Bruce held all the authority cards, but John held all the power. His message had been clearly delivered. *Fuck with me and you die.*

Bruce was shaken. Everyone in the room could sense it, almost smell the fear. It was one of John's most important and powerful weapons. Like two boxers meeting face to face, eyeball to eyeball in the center of the ring before the first bell starting the match. That's where the fight was won, long before the first bell rang.

"In New York," Bruce said. "That's where we want it done."

"Who?" John asked dryly.

"In about three weeks. The date isn't firm yet."

"Who?" John repeated.

"It needs to look like a sudden illness, an attack of some sort. Nothing violent. Nothing messy. Quiet. In his sleep kind of thing. No one to blame."

"Who?" John's impatience was beginning to surface from the sidestepping of his question.

"C-c-can… Canada. The prime minister of Canada," Andrew stammered.

"Canada?" John repeated, shocked and surprised. "Canada? The fucking prime minister of Canada? You're shitting me. We're going to war against Canada? What's wrong, are they drinking more than their share of water from Lake Erie? Or are they driving too fast down the I-87 Northway? Are you guys nuts? What the hell are you up to now? Canada for Chrissake! I don't believe this shit. Canada, what did he do to get you guys mad? Piss over Niagara Falls?"

"I thought you didn't ask why," Andrew interjected.

"The prime minister is interfering with every trade program we have with Europe and Asia," Bruce began. "He's trying to undermine our president's programs, both the new ones and the older ones already in place, and he's lining up others to support him. If he succeeds, it will greatly damage our economy and impact our trade deficits.

"The president, our president, has tried to talk to him, as have many other world leaders. He won't budge. He's trying to get all the goods coming out of Europe and Asia to be routed through a Canadian port, either on the east coast or the west, so they can be taxed when crossing the border into the U.S. He's using potential terrorist attacks on our facilities as the reason, and he's telling other countries that our ports are too corrupt to do business with.

"We all know there have been threats and at least one bombing in the port of Oakland. The result of the rerouting would be skyrocketing prices in the U.S. The price of consumer goods would go through the roof, and Canada would end up controlling our economic cash flow. He's become a dangerous man, John."

Chapter Four

"Dangerous?" John stood and paced the room in disbelief. "That's what you're calling him? Dangerous? Get a grip, people. Kill the prime minister over the price of German beer in Walmart or Italian pasta at Costco? For that, this guy deserves to die? Get a fucking grip! Are you guys serious? Who the hell came up with this brilliant idea?"

Andrew interrupted his rant. "John, you said you never ask why. Well, Bruce just told you why. You've simply got to do your job. It's been discussed and reviewed and debated at the highest levels. Every scenario, every alternative has been played out. Months of study and consideration for the consequences have been examined. It's been decided. There's a job to do. Our job. Are you going to do it or turn it down? It's as simple as that."

"Simple? So, just run out and kill the prime minister of our neighboring country! For God and country, is that it? If it's so simple, why am I here? You do it. You figure out how to get close to him. If it's so fucking simple, you don't need me, you do it."

"We know it will be difficult," Andrew continued. "That's why the job is so lucrative for you."

John paced the full length of the room. Back and forth, not looking at anyone or anything except the concrete floor. His mind was spinning, not over the assignment, but over the reason. There had to be more to this. There had to be a much deeper reason for this, something more than a trade issue. This smelled like it was personal.

"Why haven't we seen more of this in the press?" he asked. "I don't recall seeing a single report on any of the news shows about this problem. And who is going to replace him in Ottawa? Another loyal Canadian who will pick up right where he left off with the same policies? What then, kill him too?" He knew it was a question that would go unanswered.

Three sets of eyes followed his every step, not knowing what to expect. The room suddenly got very small and very warm. Each minute seemed like an hour.

"Fifty million," he said quietly.

"*What?*" Bruce blurted out.

"Fifty million," John repeated in a calm voice laced with an air of arrogance owned only by those who knew they had won the match before the first bell had sounded.

"Fifty million? Are you out of your fucking mind? Are you crazy?" Bruce shouted.

"Make it seventy-five! And please Bruce, watch your language, there's a lady in the room, and you're embarrassing me," John mocked.

"John," Andrew stepped in, attempting to calm the situation with his soft, professional voice. "You know we can't come up with seventy-five million dollars."

"I do?"

Bruce flopped down in one of the chairs, letting out a big sigh of exasperation.

"No, I don't," John continued. "You came in here with twenty-five million in your pocket. Why not seventy-five?

Why not more? In fact, let's make it a hundred. One hundred million dollars. Nice number."

"Thirty-five!" Bruce offered.

"Sixty-five," John answered calmly.

"Forty!" from Bruce.

"Fifty!" from John. "I like that number. That's a good number. Fifty or I'm out of here," he continued, a mocking sneer painted across his face.

After a long pause. "Fifty!" from Andrew.

"Done!" John replied, knowing that if he walked away from this assignment, he would become a target for elimination himself. "In advance. Transfer funds to my usual account, plus an additional one and a half in cash for expenses, handed to me in small bills no bigger than fifties. Kristin has my account number just in case you've misplaced it. I want the extra one and a half in my hands by noon tomorrow. I don't make the first move on this assignment until I get confirmation of the transfer and have the cash in hand. And finally, I'll be needing some new documents."

"You bastard!" Bruce spat out.

In what seemed a single stride, John was eye to eye with Bruce, their noses almost, but not quite, touching. His stare gripped the throat of the sitting man until he could barely breathe. "You bet I'm a bastard, you little piece of shit! And you bastards are the ones who made me who I am while sitting behind your big desks never getting your hands dirty.

"Remember? It was you who recruited me and if I wasn't good at it, we wouldn't be meeting here planning to carry out your little game of popping off the leader of our closest ally. And if you open your mouth again, the price goes back to seventy-five, and I'll do you for free. Tell the president it's a gift from me—a twofer."

The blood drained from Bruce's face as if his throat had been cut. He knew he was facing one of the deadliest men in the world. "And no refunds. From this moment on, it's a sealed deal. If you clowns have a change of heart and decide to call this off at any time before it's done, tough shit. No refunds and I'm gone. Got it, Brucie?"

"Y-y-y-yeah."

"Good!"

Chapter Five

For the next several hours, they discussed schedules and itineraries of the Canadian prime minister, covering the information available from the Canadian press. It was known that he would be visiting New York City to attend an international conference at the United Nations. His hotel and embassy were covered, as well as travel routes and other stops currently listed in his itinerary.

John did not and would not reveal his plans. He would accept the overall guidelines being laid out and the information being provided, but the final details were in his hands and only in his hands. He would reject any must-do times or places imposed upon him and would strongly suspect anyone who tried to impose them. In his mind, such demands were little more than traps where he could be set up to be caught or killed.

No! From this meeting forward, the entire mission would be in his hands. His plans, his time table, his place and his method. The method! That too would be up to him. If he felt threatened in any way, he would simply walk away. If he sensed anyone else was involved or anyone was watching him, he would simply walk away. If he saw the same strange face twice in the same place, he would simply walk away. And he made all this crystal clear to both Bruce and Andrew. The job would be done. That's all they needed to know.

He now had two missions. The same two common to all his assignments. Success and survival. He would complete his mission and he would walk away from it in one piece. Those were the two thoughts that ran through his mind as he and Kristin left the house on the hillside shortly after dark.

The other two would stay behind and "clean" the house, to be sure that no trace of their presence was left behind. The new owners would be moving in the day after tomorrow and would never be aware of what had just taken place in their dream house. They would never know that an international assassination had been planned in their basement.

With few words passing between them, Kristin drove south on I-83 to its southern end in the center of the city of Baltimore. She then zigzagged through the local streets past the aquarium and past Camden Yards until she reached the ramp leading to I-95. She repeatedly checked her rearview mirror as she drove block by block through the local traffic to see if anyone was following them.

"Did you know what the mission was?" John asked her in a cold measured tone.

"No!" she answered.

"Why not?"

"I think that's obvious. I think they knew I would resist and have as many or more questions than you had. I was told to call you in for the meeting and that was all I was told."

"Strange."

"You can say that again, but now that we know what they want you to do, it explains why I was kept in the dark."

"What do you think of the whole thing?"

"Not for me to think about it. It's up to you."

"Yeah, I know. But, I'd like you to speak your mind. Might help me understand this assignment."

"I think it stinks! I think this whole trade thing is contrived. I think there's something else behind all of this."

"Couldn't agree with you more. Two things are crystal clear to me. I don't think they ever intended to pay me. Second, whether I accepted or rejected the assignment, I'm next on their hit list. They can't risk me bouncing around the world with twenty-five mil in my pocket, potentially exposing or blackmailing them once the deed is done."

"Fifty mil!" Kristin corrected.

"Yeah, fifty mil. That really seals the deal for me. There's more to this than meets the eye and before it's done, I'll get to the bottom of it."

"But that's the why you never ask about," she said.

"Yeah! I know," he whispered to the side window.

Kristin drove past the intersection of I-95 and I-495. Neither had spoken for some time.

"Where to now, boss lady?"

"My place."

"Um, I thought we tried that once already today?"

"Oh no! That was only a teaser. Now that we have this thing in our laps, we go to the real 'my place.' The place where I sleep."

"Okay, but why there, boss?"

"Like I said, because that's where I sleep."

"And where exactly is it that you're taking me?"

"Like I said, to my place."

"Your place?"

"Yup!"

"You and me?"

"Yup!" The banter continued.

"Isn't that sort of crossing some kind of invisible line, boss lady?"

"Yup!"

"And that's okay?"

Chapter Five

"Yup!"

"How come?"

"Well, because it's been quite awhile since I last saw you. And because I've been wanting to be with you since the first time I met you. And because you are one hot dude. And because I've never slept with a man who just made fifty million dollars."

"Fifty-one and a half!" he corrected.

"Right. Even better!"

"And you want me to believe that's the real reason?"

"Yup!"

"What about the line we're about to cross?"

"The only line I see is that white one in the road. And besides, fifty-one and a half million dollars—that's a big eraser." She looked over at him with a sexy grin dripping from her face like sweet milk chocolate.

They drove a few minutes without saying anything more. Then John asked, "How much did he walk in there with?"

"Thirty-five million plus another half for expenses."

"Good! That means I stuck it to them."

"And then some. You picked them clean. Neither of them may hold onto their job with that price tag. They'll have to really dance to get it approved. Does that make you feel good?"

"Yup!"

"A small victory?"

"Big... small... doesn't matter. A victory is a victory and any size will do just fine when I win against pompous bureaucratic asses like those two. And I also beat their bosses, all the way up the line. They'll have to go to the big guy to get that amount approved.

"Yeah. It's worth it," he continued. "They play with lives, Kristin, as if they were toy trucks in a sandbox. Move one here. Crash one there. They see no blood. Never feel any pain. Never smell any fear. Their hands are always in their pockets, nice and warm and clean. They never look into the eye of a man who is about to die. The man they ordered to die. Never see the fear when he knows he is about to take his last breath."

"Just like a general in the military."

"No, Kristin. A general isn't born a general. He comes up through the ranks. He earns his stars. Generals pay the price just like the grunts in the trenches. Generals got to be generals because somewhere along the line, somebody was shooting at them. Generals started off as lieutenants. These guys ride the shirttails of some hotshot, silver-tongued, photogenic rich-boy-turned-politician and get appointed to a high-paying job as a reward for a fat contribution their daddy made; they haven't got the slightest fucking idea what's really going on. All they see is power. They measure everything in dollars. Dollars and power.

Chapter Five

"They have no idea what it costs the guys they send me out to get. They have no idea about the families left alone. And they don't care. And they have no idea what it costs me! Inside me. My mind. My spirit. My soul. And they don't care. Just themselves. That's all that matters to them.

"They play chess with other countries, puffing up their egos, getting caught up in the power trip until they believe the world revolves around their big fat asses. They're on a rocket ride to a distant star that they see as their righteous place in history when it's really a ride to hell. They don't see that they are punching their own ticket to hell. They're too arrogant to see it. Blinded by the light of their own star.

"Every four years, here they come. As predictable as a fart after eating a can of beans. The next generation of egos thinking they can do more and do it better than the last batch of rocket riders. They just keep coming.

"Take a look at the bunch we have in the White House right now. Smarter than anybody that's been there before them. Just ask; they'll tell you without a doubt. Damned fools! They graduate as snot-nosed students from Yale and Harvard and Princeton—power hungry jerks wearing out the carpets in the White House.

"Every four years, the first Tuesday of November, a new crop comes in and the old crop joins the Meet-the-Press club. Their power is gone, but their egos live on. The circle is closed.

"And then, when the new group of twelve-year-old geniuses get their boss's tit caught in a wringer because they couldn't figure out which way Thursday morning was, they call on a jerk like me to do their dirty work. When something or someone gets in their way, becomes an obstacle to the world seeing how wonderful and smart they are, my phone rings and they want me to come help them polish their star."

He paused, realizing he had been talking non-stop, venting his inner tension to the beautiful woman sitting next to him.

"Sorry I'm ranting, but yeah! Kristin. A little victory goes a long way. To squeeze a few bucks extra, to make them squirm and have them go back to their boss on their knees, to have to admit that they failed even if it was just a little bit, yeah, it helps. At least I get to feel that I've kept the zookeeper in the cage even if for just a little bit."

She listened without interrupting. He had to vent, to cleanse himself. A verbal catharsis. How many years, how many missions had this been building? She knew there was more. She knew that way down deep there was a lot more that he would never let a stranger hear. Or admit to himself. With no one to vent to, no one to trust, no one close to him. He had been alone for so many years. And now...

She also knew that there was more to the man, more than anyone really knew. She knew he was not just a mind-less, unfeeling killer. She had worked with him, if only at a distance, for years. She had studied him. Read and reread his file repeatedly. All the history and all the data ever gathered on him before he was recruited and every word since. She had studied every assignment, every step, his methods, his behavior, his profile. Everything she could gather from his childhood until this very moment.

She knew him, knew him better than he knew himself. And she knew what drove him. She could reread his file far easier than he could relive the events she had access to. What made him tick! What kept him going! She had to. She had to know him well enough to ask him to kill, and to control him while he went about his business. It was her job.

They had met face to face so few times over the years, but she was connected to him in so many ways. From the first time she met him, she felt they were somehow linked, a great match, spiritually, psychologically, emotionally, and the link between them had grown stronger with every mission she had to ask him to complete.

In her own way, she was with him every moment. She knew how he did his work and when it was done. She knew what he did and how he had done it. But she didn't know why. Why does a man kill another man? Willingly and voluntarily, seemingly without concern or feeling remorse. Was it simply for the money? She didn't believe that. Didn't *want* to believe that. There had to be something else.

Money couldn't be the only reason. But if it wasn't, what was? She couldn't accept that he would lower himself to killing another human being just to be paid. There was too much to the man. There had to be some driving motive she hadn't yet found, or come to understand.

Even though she was confined to an office, she was with him when she knew he was in danger. He was ordered to call her at the completion of each assignment to report the status of the mission and on his condition. She somehow knew it was him before she even picked up the phone. She would snatch the telephone up before the first ring was complete. She would listen to him report that everything was okay, that he was okay.

She would listen to his voice, not just his words, listen to the tone and inflection to hear the real report. She would feel the pain and the hurt along with him, and on the rare occasion that he had been injured, she would bleed with him. She sensed the toll each mission took on him.

He was a killer. A hired, methodical, professional killer. He would seek out the prey assigned to him, total strangers, men he had never met, who had never done anything to him, men who had never touched his life in any way. He would seek them out, stalk them, observe and study them, all for one purpose: to plan their death. How he would end a life. How he would kill them. And how he would walk away, seemingly unaffected.

And yet, alone with him in her car, knowing what he was, what he did, knowing that in an instant he could kill her in a dozen different ways, she was not afraid. Strangely, she felt...safe ...protected. She did not feel threatened in any way by him.

Why? Was it animal magnetism? The mystery of it? No, that was not the feeling she was experiencing, not the emotions running through her body. Then what? What the hell was it?

Did she have to admit to herself that she simply wanted him that badly? That she wanted to rip his clothes off and have raw, naked sex with him because he was a dangerous killer? Was that the attraction? Flirting with the danger of being in the hands, in the control of a killer?

Or was it something else? Was it the warmth of him that she sensed would come after the physical sex? Was it the finding of the key to unlock him? To reach inside him?

Chapter Five

It was not smart trying to get close to this man. It was stupid. Getting close to him could get them both killed. She wanted him for all the wrong reasons. He was a myth. He was smoke. She couldn't possibly be in love with him. His voice intruded into her churning mind.

"Drop me off here."

"What?"

"Drop me off here."

"But why?"

"I've got work to do."

"Now?"

"Yes."

"But—"

"Kristin, you're a beautiful woman, and very sexy. I'd love to go home with you tonight— or any night. We could have a quiet dinner and make love until the sun came up. And I hope someday we will do just that. But not now. Not tonight."

"Why— why not?"

"Because I've got work to do. And besides, I'd be putting you in danger."

"Danger?"

"Yes."

"How?"

"Does Bruce know where you live?"

"Well, yes. At least he has my address. It's in my file. He's never been to my apartment. Andrew has. He picked me up one day on our way to the airport."

"And I'll bet that was within the last week or two, right?"

"Y-y-yes. But how did you know?"

"Trust me, I know. Look in your rearview mirror."

She followed his instructions with a puzzled look sliding down her face.

"See that little red sports car?"

"Yes," she answered softly, her voice weak and shaky.

"How many turns have you made since we got off the interstate?"

"I don't know… six, maybe seven."

"So has it. And before that, there was a small blue pickup, before that, a fake taxi. The pickup and the little red car switched at the traffic light we went through when you got off the interstate."

"I don't believe it."

"You don't? Then keep driving and I'll show you. They will probably switch again soon. Close to your apartment.

Chapter Five

The last car will be a four-door sedan. Dark color. There will be two men in it, maybe three, to keep each other awake throughout the night."

"Throughout the night?"

"Yes. And I'll bet your place is wired for sound and maybe more."

"More? What do you mean, more?" her startled voice shrieked above the noise of a passing truck.

"Video. Maybe motion-activated still cameras. They need leverage. If you're going to knock off the prime minister of the country many consider to be our closest friend in the whole world, you want to be sure you have the upper hand with everyone involved and like it or not, you are involved.

"Why do you think I demanded payment in advance? Have you ever heard of anyone getting paid up front? They didn't intend to ever pay me. That's why they came in with twenty-five million in their pocket. Never intended to pay it. I would do my job and there would be someone waiting in the wings to do me immediately afterwards and then, probably to wipe the slate clean, you would be next. They couldn't leave any possibility of this ever getting out. No dangling loose ends.

"Killing our closest friend and ally? Are you kidding me? It had to end with me and unfortunately, with you. So, payment up front, and now I must take care of you as well. Now watch!"

Kristin drove another half mile before she came to one of the traffic lights on her normal route home. The red sports car pulled off to the curb and parked behind a dark blue Chevy. When the traffic light turned green, and she began to drive on, the red car stayed parked. The dark blue Chevy's headlights came on and pulled out behind her. There were two men in the front seat—and one in the rear.

"Switch," John said softly.

"Well, I'll be damned. How did you know? How did you see them doing that?"

"I stay alive by seeing things like that, remember? Now, take me to Tysons Corner and drop me off in front of the Marriott Hotel."

She turned right at the next intersection and drove west toward Tysons Corner. Ten minutes later, she pulled up in the circular drive of the hotel. The Chevy pulled into the parking lot and came to a stop facing the circle.

"Now argue with me," John directed. "Make it animated, but don't overdo it. Make it look real."

She acted with him for thirty seconds, almost laughing at the ridiculous image they must be making. "Now slap me," John ordered.

"What?"

"Slap me, and make it a good one. When I get out of the car, I'm going to slam the door hard. Real hard like I'm pissed off at you. Then you floor this buggy of yours and go straight home and go to bed. I'll contact you day after tomorrow in our usual way. It will sound like a routine check-in call.

Chapter Five

"And don't forget," he continued. "Your place is probably wired. So be careful what you say, and don't get undressed tonight without a robe close by. You might be on candid camera and I'd sure be pissed off if I missed the show. Now, slap me."

She brought her left arm back and in a wide, arching loop took a swing at him, slapping him across the face with a full open hand, rocking his head violently. He caught a glimpse of the man standing next to the dark blue Chevy; he was watching Kristin's car. John reached up to rub his tingling face and said, "That'll work! I'm sure they'll buy that one."

He reached over the front seat, grabbed his leather travel bag and roughly exited the car, slamming the door behind him. Kristin floored her gas pedal and squealed her tires as she pulled away from the hotel entrance.

"Nice work," John muttered as he watched her streak out of the hotel driveway and onto the street. He watched until her car disappeared into the local traffic headed toward D.C. The Chevy was only a couple of seconds behind, leaving the one agent observing from between two parked cars. John would have to shake him off his tail, but that would be easy enough to do.

He walked toward the front door of the hotel but didn't enter. Instead, he turned and hailed a taxi cab parked close by waiting for a customer. The cab pulled up and he got in, issuing a single command as the driver pulled away. "National," was all he had to say.

Thirty minutes later, John paid the driver for the ride to Reagan National Airport and exited the cab. A few yards behind him, a second cab was being paid. His shadow, the lone agent from the hotel, had followed him to the airport.

John walked into the terminal building with his bag and headed directly for the New York shuttle. He slipped a credit card into the vending unit, pulled out a boarding pass, turned and headed for the jetway. After passing through the security check area, he leaned up against a post and looked back toward the TSA agents checking oncoming passengers. The agent following him did not attempt to enter. Instead he reached for his cell phone and punched in numbers.

John knew that the agent would not be allowed to follow him onto the aircraft; the call was to inform his superiors of what was taking place. Another agent would be assigned to meet John on the New York end of the flight. Surprise! John wouldn't be there.

As soon as the agent turned to leave the terminal, thinking that his job was done, John also exited the New York shuttle area, returned to the ticket vending machine, and purchased a ticket for the Boston shuttle. Whoever would be waiting for him at LaGuardia would be in for a long night. He would be in Bean Town—at least temporarily.

Chapter Six

Three hours later, John was standing on the platform of Boston's South Street Amtrak station waiting for the next train to New York City. The train would pass through Rhode Island before reaching the coast of Connecticut. In Norwalk, New Haven, Bridgeport, and Stamford, the train would fill with men wearing three-piece blue uniforms and women with fat ankles jammed into overstuffed panty hose, wearing their Nike cross trainers to convince themselves they were in good physical condition, while carrying a bag with their high heels to switch into, once hidden behind their desk.

Little men in big bodies and wannabe fashion plate women with inflated salaries matching their inflated IQ's, all imitating the captains of industry riding the rails to Mecca with grim faces, wallowing in their own self-importance. A trainload of legends-in-their-own-minds spending two cents for every one that they earn, trying to impress the world and themselves with themselves.

The Salesman

John would get off the Amtrak in Stamford and switch to a Metro North commuter train into Grand Central Station, arriving at the peak of the morning rush. He knew of a mid-level hotel off the beaten path that had little lobby traffic. He did not want to stay at any of the big-name chain hotels. That's where the prime minister of Canada and all other world leaders would be staying for the United Nations conference.

The Middletown Hotel on 53rd Street off Third Avenue was perfect, a businessman's hotel within walking distance of every place he would be visiting in the next few days. John decided to walk the eleven blocks to loosen his stiff body after riding all night on airplanes and trains. He slipped the strap of his bag over one shoulder, picked up his briefcase in the opposite hand, and set out on foot.

He rode the escalator up from the main level of the world-famous train terminal, walked through what was once the Pan Am building, made famous by helicopters landing on its roof. He then walked through the Helmsley Building, emerging on the west side of Park Avenue. At the next corner, he crossed the wide avenue. When he reached the Waldorf Astoria, he entered through the revolving doors facing Park Avenue, and walked up the staircase to the main floor, stopping at the lobby lounge.

He looked back toward where he had entered the hotel to see if any face in the small crowd milling around the lobby was paying too much attention to him or trying too hard to avoid eye contact. Seeing none, he continued across the lobby and exited the hotel onto Lexington Avenue. He turned to his left to continue north toward 53rd Street.

When he reached the Middletown Hotel, he approached the front desk. Using his best fake British accent, he spoke to the clerk. "Good morning, I was told that you might have a room available with a kitchenette."

"Yes, sir. We have accommodations available. How long will you be staying with us?"

"Approximately a week. Perhaps a bit longer." He produced a European credit card, and a British passport and credit card, all in the name of Richard F. Kirkpatrick.

"The rate is $185.00 per night, sir. Will that be satisfactory?"

"Yes, thank you," he answered, as snobbishly as his English accent could muster.

Within a few minutes, he was safely in his room. It was approaching 10:00 a.m. A shower and a few hours of sleep were next on his agenda. He was tired. His mind hadn't stopped working for a moment since he left the Baltimore meeting with Kristin and the two agents. On top of the assignment handed to him, the ride and conversation with Kristin swirled around in his head. He needed some rest.

What puzzled him most was why he was being followed? Not only was it highly unusual, it was dangerous, dangerous for all involved. It could potentially expose him and his assignment. It was also dangerous to those trying their best to keep tabs on him. Bruce knew better. He knew that he worked alone.

Bruce also knew that John was their most successful agent, or he wouldn't have been chosen for this assignment, that he had stayed alive as long as he had because he was extremely good at what he did— including detecting anyone trying to follow him.

Most of all, Bruce knew that if he felt threatened by another agent's exposing him and putting his life at risk, the agent's own life was in danger. John would kill him if it interfered with his success or threatened his survival. So, why?

He needed rest more than he had anticipated. He slept until nearly 5:30 p.m. When he woke, he showered again to refresh himself and be alert. He dressed and walked across town to the Cattleman's Club Restaurant, where he had a great steak dinner, followed by an equally great cigar, courtesy of the house, an old tradition the establishment had followed for many years, and with a hundred bucks for dinner, a tradition they could afford.

After dinner, he casually walked back to his hotel, arriving close to 10:00 p.m. Every step along the way his training and experience demanded that he observe every face around him. Every reflection in every window. Every scent and sight, every expression on every face that might indicate someone had more interest in him than warranted by a stranger passing on a quiet New York City sidewalk late in the evening.

Every automobile, every license plate, every taxi cab, every van bearing lettering on its side. So far—nothing. He was satisfied he was indeed alone. This was the best time in Manhattan. The craziness of the business day was over. The rush of traffic and the accompanying noise it generated settled down, and the streets took on a sense of quiet. People returned to humanity, only to leave it again early the following morning.

As he sat quietly in his room, he had to fight off the thought of the millions of dollars now resting in his bank account. He had gotten online as soon as he returned to his room to verify that the deposit had been made. The sum kept creeping into his mind as he thought of what he had forced from Bruce and his bosses. What would the price of this money be to them? What were the consequences of his demands? What would he pay for sticking it to all the ego-crats all the way up to, and including the Oval Office?

He immediately wired instructions to the bank to transfer his entire account balance less one dollar to yet another account in another part of the world. He didn't trust Bruce and believed that they would ultimately attempt to kill him and retrieve the money. So, he took measured steps to shake them off the money trail.

He couldn't allow himself to think about the massive amount just sitting there waiting for him to spend. He wouldn't allow himself to think of it as a fee to kill. He didn't think of himself as just a killer for hire. If he did, his next victim would be himself. As self-serving as it might be, he considered himself a soldier and justified his actions as those of a patriot doing a job his country needed done to be safe. Secure. To be free. He was a soldier without a uniform. He was fighting a war that had no defined battle-field, and few rules.

He was repulsed by killing, by death. It appealed to him in the same way the job of opening a septic tank to clean it out with a bucket would appeal to him. No matter how you did it, it stunk and you would be covered with shit.

It was a job! He got paid a lot of money because of the personal risk and sacrifice that went along with his assignments. He was convinced that if he didn't do the job, someone else would. Someone with less honor. Someone cold-blooded, out for only the money. Someone for sale to the highest bidder, someone with the wrong motives.

Killing wasn't his purpose in life. Freedom was. The protection of democracy was. All the things that those who sent him out on these assignments seemed to have forgotten. All those pretending to be leaders, jealous of the greatness of those they were supposed to be serving.

He hated them, hated what they did. Hated what they asked him to do! He knew that death was sometimes a way, maybe the only way, to solve a major problem. But it was never easy. Should never be easy. Little by little, it was destroying him. He grew more and more angry with himself and the world he lived in. Maybe the fifty million would be his last fee. Maybe this was his last assignment. Maybe...

He sat in his room watching television until almost 1:30 in the morning, flipping through the channels. From CNN to ESPN to Fox News and back again. Story after story of death and murder and corruption and hunger followed by greedy, snot-nosed 22-year-old kids signing multimillion dollar contracts to play a game.

His anger grew as he watched these pompous athletes strut and pose in their Nike gear, justifying every penny they were getting, boasting how wonderful they were and how beautiful they were, while the next channel showed kids living in huts, dying of starvation and disease. *What a fucked-up world,* he thought.

Then he thought of the millions of dollars he now had sitting in a bank and how hypocritical he was being, how he was a part of the same world he hated watching. The thought festered in his mind and suddenly, for the first time, he knew what he would do with all that money once this assignment was all over and done with. He now knew it would be his last.

The thought suddenly blossomed in his brain, and he knew he had a purpose, an objective, a reason for what he was doing. He wanted to share this. All of this. Not just the money, but the whole idea that took shape in his mind. He wanted to share it with someone. But who? Who? And then he realized that the only person entering his mind was Kristin. Kristin Blake!

Chapter Seven

The next morning he walked the streets of midtown Manhattan for over six hours. He knew the area well, having studied it for other assignments in the past.

Bruce and Andrew told him that the prime minister's death was to look like a natural event, not an assassination. No long-range rifle shot from a strategic location. No double-tap head shots in an elevator or while he was asleep in his hotel room. No well-placed knife or other weapon into a vital body organ while he walked the streets of Manhattan.

Natural causes…no poison…no suffocating. No fall from a window. The possible methods grew ever more limited. Chemically induced heart failure with an untraceable substance. Okay, but how? How would he get it into the prime minister's body? Not by injection, obviously. It would have to be ingested—in food or drink.

A plan began to form in his mind. He walked over to the east side toward the United Nations building, then back west toward Grand Central Station and on farther west to Times Square. Then north on Eighth Avenue toward Columbus Circle and Central Park.

All the while, he was thinking of only one thing. A way out, an escape route. The only purpose of this was to find a back door. Once the prime minister went down, even though it looked to be of natural causes, the New York City Police would shut down all escape routes from Manhattan Island. Twelve miles long and two and a half miles wide… it would become a prison. They would close down all the tunnels and bridges and ferries connecting the island to the surrounding boroughs and New Jersey.

The plan to kill was forming in his head as he walked. The plan to escape was far more complex. There were ways and routes he could take, but timing would be everything. It would take the NYPD only minutes to close all the escape routes: the George Washington Bridge, the Lincoln and Holland Tunnels, all crossings to Brooklyn and Queens, the ferry to Staten Island, and the northern bridges to the Bronx.

So what was left? No boat would be allowed to leave any of the few marinas servicing Manhattan. It was impossible to swim across the East River because of the swift current, and the Hudson River was way too wide to even consider. Walking across one of the bridges to Brooklyn, as did so many on September 11, 2001, only put him onto another island prison. Long Island was much bigger, but an island none the less.

Think!

He looked at his watch. Time to call in. Time to set yet another piece of his plan into motion. His call was answered between the first and second ring.

"Hello!"

"Kristin, hi Baby, it's Dad!" A brief moment of hesitation. She had never heard this greeting from him before.

"Hi, Daddy! How are you?"

"I'm fine, Baby, and how are you?"

"I'm fine. Are you at home?" *Mission location.*

"Yeah. Got here late yesterday. Got delayed leaving. Would you believe that two rodents somehow got into my rental car? I was parked next to a big garbage dumpster. I had to get rid of them before I turned it in. And on top of that, I had to switch planes at the last minute. First flight was overbooked. Too much of a crowd." *His message was being delivered to all who might be listening. He also knew he had revealed that he was in New York City.*

"Dad, I have a package for you. It was left at your front door while you were away. I picked it up for safekeeping. How would you like for me to get it to you?" *She had his million and a half expense money.*

"Hmm. I have an idea. Why don't you bring it over to me tonight? Say, around six. I'll buy you dinner, and we can get caught up on things. You can take the Metro here, and then I'll drive you home." *Come to New York City tonight on the 6:00 pm train.*

"I-I— I don't know if I can do that." *She was not permitted to go into the field.*

"Sure you can. As a matter of fact, I insist. And be sure to bring the package with you. Oh— and why don't you bring some clothes with you and stay the night? There's a sleeper couch in my room we can use. That way we don't have to worry about getting you home too late, and we can have a nice long visit." *You come, bring the money, and plan on staying.*

"Dad, I don't— hold on a minute, someone just walked into my office." *Andrew had come into her office.* "Daddy, I don't think I can do that. I have an early morning meeting that—"

"But I insist. It's been too long since we had some private time together. If you don't come, I'll die of a broken heart." *You will come, you will bring the money, you will come alone or someone might get hurt.*

There was a short silence; he was sure Andrew was giving her instructions. John was absolutely sure they were monitoring his conversation with Kristin. "Well, okay Daddy. If you insist. I guess I can be there."

"Great! I'll meet you at the house. See you around six." *Message delivered. Plan continues.* He had a lot to do and he needed to get to it.

At 5:45 that afternoon, Kristin exited a car driven by her boss. She took a short walk into Union Station in the heart of Washington, D.C. She made her way to the ticket counter and purchased a one-way ticket that would take her through Baltimore, Philadelphia and on to Penn

Station in New York City. The ride would take a little more than three hours.

She knew from John's coded conversation, *I'll meet you at the house,* that he planned on meeting her at the station. She had only a small overnight bag with her containing toiletry items and enough clothes to last for a day or two. She anticipated that she would be returning to D.C. as soon as she turned over the satchel of expense money to John.

She was very nervous carrying a bag full of cash. Who wouldn't be? She felt as if she had a big neon sign hanging on her chest flashing out the message: "I'm carrying a million and a half dollars in cash. Come and get it!"

She found a seat on the train, placed her travel bag in the overhead rack, and stowed the satchel of money under her legs. She snuggled down, opened a magazine, and pretended to be reading while she searched the entire car for anything that looked troublesome. This was her first experience out of her office, and she suddenly became aware of what John's life must be like every day of the year. She felt sure that she was being followed and watched by someone working for Bruce. She felt naked.

Three hours and ten minutes later, the train pulled into Penn Station. She got up and began walking toward the front end of the car to exit onto the platform. A short distance from where she stepped onto the platform, there was a narrow single-person-wide escalator that would bring her up to the main level of the terminal. As she neared the top of the escalator, she felt a slight nudge in her back and a familiar voice.

"Don't look back. You are being followed. Turn left when you reach the main level and head for the 34th Street exit. Then walk across the street and go into Macy's. Find the ladies shoe department and pretend you're buying something until I come and get you."

The pressure on her back disappeared, and so did the voice. When she reached the main level, she paused to read the overhead signs and followed them toward 34th street. Suddenly, she heard a commotion behind her and a dog barking. She had passed a uniformed U.S. Customs officer holding a dog on a leash as she walked across the main lobby. She guessed it was a drug-sniffing dog and that it had detected someone.

She exited the station and crossed the street into the iconic department store. She had never seen anything like it in Washington; she'd only seen the store on television when the Thanksgiving Day parade was telecast. It was far more impressive up-front and personal.

She entered through one of the revolving doors and began walking through the merchandise displays. Before she could find the shoe department, she felt a hand firmly, but gently, grip her elbow.

"Keep walking. I think I've diverted them, but we need to be sure."

She looked up to see the face of a strange man with dark-rimmed glasses, a bulky raincoat, a bushy mustache, and equally bushy eyebrows. Half of his face was covered with mutton chop sideburns.

"You— you were on the train! I saw you standing near the men's room at the end of the car."

"Yeah! That was me. Keep moving. There were three people following you. I took care of one in the station, but the other two made it to the street."

He guided her to the elevators near the center of the store and pushed the buttons for every floor. Only a young woman with her two small children entered before the door slid closed. They rode the elevator to the third floor before getting off. John then held Kristin by the arm and stood at the door to the car right next to the one they had just exited. When it arrived from the upper floors, they stepped in and rode it back down to the main floor. He held her back and to the side as the door opened, so he could look out to see if anyone was there who might be following them.

He did not see either of the two remaining faces from the train. Once again, taking her by the arm, he led her back out onto the sidewalk and started walking toward the Empire State Building. On the corner of 34th street and Seventh Avenue, he hailed a taxi and the two of them got in as quickly as they could.

"Port Authority Terminal please, driver," was his command.

"John, you—"

"Shhhh… Not now. Wait a bit and we'll talk." He nodded his head toward the cab driver.

Fifteen minutes later, the taxi pulled up in front of the largest bus terminal in the world. They got out of the cab at the Eighth Avenue entrance and he led her inside. It was crowded, as it was almost twenty-four hours a day, with commuters coming from and going to every corner of the vast metropolitan area of New York City, Long Island, New Jersey, Connecticut and beyond.

He led her to the north side of the terminal and exited on the 41st Street side, immediately crossing the street and heading east toward Times Square. They walked two blocks before they ducked into the set-back entryway of a store selling cheap luggage.

John surveyed everyone coming and going on the street until he was satisfied that they had lost the man and woman who had accompanied Kristin on her train ride from Washington.

"Have you got any cash on you?" he asked, while still looking out at the street.

"John, I'm carrying a million and a half dollars in cash, remember?"

"Right. Slipped my mind. Here, take this. It's the key to my hotel room with the name and address on it. Walk to the corner and get a cab. Tell the driver to take you to the hotel. It's only about a five-minute ride. When you get there, give him twenty bucks no matter what the fare is. It should be less, but a big tip goes a long way in this town. When you get there, go up to the room and lock the door behind you. Don't open it for anyone. I'll be there as soon as possible."

He stood next to her as she got into a taxi, and it pulled away from the curb, blending into the crosstown traffic. Within a block, it disappeared into the sea of yellow vehicles that flooded this part of the city. He stepped back against the building and watched the actions of the people walking nearby. Seeing nothing of concern after ten minutes, he turned and started walking back to the Port Authority Bus Terminal.

It took him about twenty minutes to spot the faces he was looking for. He had seen the woman before the train trip. She had also been acting as a car rental agent behind the counter at the airport when he first arrived in Baltimore.

The two were now wandering around the terminal searching faces in the hope of picking up his trail. Instead, he had picked up theirs. It was time to put this little game to rest. Relying on the disguise he had been wearing since he took the afternoon train, he approached the two agents. He stepped between the two, grabbing each at the back of the neck, temporarily immobilizing them.

"I told Bruce not to have her followed," he said quietly as he pulled their heads close to him.

"What? Who are you?"

John released them both and stood directly in front of the male agent, placing his hand in his pocket as if holding a gun.

"I have a gun aimed right at your balls, so if you don't want to sing soprano for the rest of your life, the two of you turn toward the exit and start walking."

The two agents stood still, staring at the man in front of them, trying to make out who was talking to them.

"*Move!*" John ordered.

Chapter Seven

Finally realizing who was ordering them, they turned and began walking toward the Eighth Avenue exit of the terminal.

"Get on the taxi line," John ordered.

It took a couple of minutes for them to progress to the front of the line. When it was their turn to enter a cab, John said, "You two take this cab back to Penn Station and hop the next train back to D.C. You can deliver this message to your boss: Next time I see someone on my tail, they will be riding back in a body bag.

"The NYPD should be releasing your buddy by now. I slipped that marijuana joint into his pocket for the dog to sniff out. The customs agent was just doing his job. Now get in and don't try to come back this way. I'll be gone before you reach the corner.

"And tell Bruce, I have a body bag reserved for him if I even smell anyone on me. Got it?"

They nodded, following his directions without a word. Within a few seconds, they were clear of the terminal, with the cab cutting across Eighth Avenue to turn right onto 42nd street to return to Penn Station. As soon as the cab blended into the traffic, John turned and reentered the terminal building to once more lose himself in the crowd, should they attempt to return to follow him.

He didn't think they would risk it. They knew who he was and what his reputation was. He was sure he had scared them enough to take a train back to D.C.

Less than an hour after putting Kristin in the taxi, John was gently knocking on the door to his hotel room.

He could see the shadow of her face moving across the peephole in the door before she was sliding the chain lock and pulling back the dead bolt. She opened the door and fell into his arms.

"Oh my God! I was so worried. I was scared to death."

"It's okay. I took care of them and all is clear now."

"How?"

"I just walked up to them and suggested they catch the next train back to D.C. and leave us to have a quiet evening together. They smiled and were delighted that we were having a good time here in the Big Apple and wished us well."

"You're full of shit, John. Did you have to hurt them?"

"Is that any way for a lady to talk? No, I didn't hurt them."

She crossed the room and sat on the edge of the bed. "What now?" she asked.

"Now we find out what the hell is going on."

Chapter Eight

"Are you hungry?" he asked.

"Starving!"

"Okay, I know a place less than a block from here where we can get a late dinner and a drink. New York City never sleeps."

They walked to the restaurant and ordered their meals. John could see the nervousness in Kristin. She was tense and fidgety, picking up her utensils and rearranging them on her napkin over and over. He finally reached across the table and took her by the hand.

"Calm down, little lady. You're all right now. They weren't out to harm either of us. They were just following us, checking up on me."

She took a deep breath, let it out with a slow sigh, and looked at him. "Why were they following me? How did you know? When did you get on the train? How did you spot them?"

The nervous questions poured out of her. John put his finger to his lips.

"Shh. Take it easy. I'll explain everything. Try to enjoy your drink and relax."

"What do we do now?"

"Enjoy dinner and each other's company."

An hour later, after a bottle of wine, they were walking back toward the hotel. John reached out and took Kristin by the hand, more to reassure her than as a romantic gesture.

"Here's what I think is going on, Kristin. There's more to this thing than we know."

"Why do you say that?"

"Well, to me it's quite obvious. Let's start at the beginning. First, I'm not the kind of agent who gets summoned in from the field for a face-to-face meeting. You know that very well. I get assignments, and I carry them out with minimum risk of exposure. End of story.

"Second, twenty-five million dollars as an opener? Come on! My usual payment is a couple of hundred thousand maybe, and half a million for a really big deal. And then to cave on my counter of fifty million? Sure, Bruce put up a struggle, but in the end, he caved. Something is very wrong with that. Approval for that amount had to come from way up the ladder." He paused, then added, "Way up!

"I don't think they ever intended to pay me, and I don't think that either of us was ever intended to survive this assignment. That's why I insisted on your bringing me the expense money. I needed to get you away from them."

"You really think they were going to kill me?"

"Kristin, I've been at this game a long time. Longer than most in this business. I can smell a rat a long way off. That's why I'm still alive. This rat stinks to high heaven. And first trying to tail me after the meeting, followed by tailing you to get back on my trail? All very bad signs and very stupid. They know, or at least should have known, that they would never get away with it.

"I felt sure they would try that, so I took an early train back to D.C. to watch over you and see what they might be up to. I immediately spotted the three of them, and that confirmed my suspicions. Something's rotten about this whole deal. So, to answer your question, now we find out what's going on."

"How?"

"I need to sleep on it. I'll have it figured out in the morning. We have some time. The U.N. conference isn't for another eight days, so it will be a week before the prime minister arrives in New York."

"What about—?"

"Don't worry, I'll sleep on the couch."

"Not if I have anything to say about it."

They returned to the hotel room, desire and lust mounting between them in untamed, uncontrollable passion. They attacked each other like two starving dogs on raw meat, falling into bed and pulling off each other's clothes.

He entered her and she accepted him so willingly, so quickly, that it seemed as if this were the hundredth time they were together instead of the first. Raw sex has only one successful outcome and they found it within minutes. Their union was a combination of lust and love driven by the mountain of tension both felt. The past few days had concentrated their act into an explosion.

John woke up at ten minutes after six in the morning. He went into the kitchenette, found the courtesy coffee packets, and made a pot, his mind racing from the events of the previous day. One thing he knew for sure: last evening had not been a one-night stand. As raw as it was, this woman had reached something inside him that went far beyond the lust of casual sex.

He knew he was taking on a new responsibility. His life had become more complicated. He had to take care of her, to protect her. Her job exposed her to the dangers ahead, but it was his actions that would cement her doom. Or not. He was responsible for dragging her into this. Now it was up to him to see that she— that *they* survived.

"Good morning," he heard her say from across the room. She sat up in bed with the sheet pulled up to cover her breasts, her luxurious hair flowing over her shoulders. Her voice melted him.

Chapter Eight

"Good morning! Coffee?"

"Please. Black."

"Coming up."

He reached across the counter for a second mug and filled it with freshly-brewed coffee. He walked over and sat on the edge of the bed. They sipped the hot brew in silence. There were two three-hundred-pound gorillas in the room. One was their time together in the bed they sat on, and the second was the big question: What's next?

Kristin broke the silence. "What now, John?"

"Well, we could order breakfast from room service and kick back and enjoy the day here in the room…"

"Or?"

He let out a deep sigh. "Or, we could get the hell out of here and try to find out exactly what's going on with this screwed up assignment I've been given."

"How do we do that?"

"First, I get you to a place where you'll be safe until I get to the bottom of things."

"And then?"

"And then I'm not quite sure. I have a lot buzzing around in my head. And I'm hungry. What would you like for breakfast?"

"You!"

They fell back into bed. However, this was not physical sex. This time their union was soft and tender and loving. Touching with finger tips and moist lips. Their eyes never left each other's. He entered her gently, moving slowly. She held him close to her, enjoying his warmth. There was no urgency to their movements, and when they neared satisfaction, it was their hearts that reached for ecstasy.

After showering and dressing, they packed what little they had with them, including the satchel of cash, placing everything in the closet, the cash in the room safe. They would return after breakfast to retrieve their meager belongings. Once out on the sidewalk in front of the hotel, John was about to hail a taxi. Instead, he took Kristin firmly by the arm and led her away from the hotel entrance. She looked up at him, wondering what he was doing.

"John, you're hurting me. You're hurting my arm."

"Listen to me very carefully. I want you to walk straight ahead. Don't look back, don't look over your shoulder. Turn left at the corner and walk until you reach 48th street. Then turn right until you reach Park Avenue. Across the avenue, you will see a black building, number 250 Park. Walk into the lobby. On the left there is a bank. On the right is a concession stand. Find a place in the lobby where you can see the entrance to both and wait there for me. Do you understand?"

"Yes, but why? What's going on?"

"We're being followed."

"What! Where? Who?"

Chapter Eight

"There are two people across the street standing in front of the little coffee shop. A man and a woman. Not the same pair that were on the train yesterday— the man acting as the conductor taking tickets and the woman sitting across from you knitting with a bag of yarn in her lap.

"What do we do?"

"You keep walking. I'll be there as soon as I can. They will follow me, not you. I'm the one they've been assigned to watch and figure out what I'm up to."

"But—"

"Just do it…and wait for me. If anyone approaches you and tries to take you away, scream your head off. Got it?"

"Yes!"

He released her arm and gave her a mock farewell. He stood in place until she had reached the street corner and turned as he had instructed her. The man and woman watching them made no attempt to follow her. He turned around and walked toward the East River. He wanted to lead them away from Kristin.

At the corner, he waved down a taxi. He intentionally got into the cab, moving slowly to allow the two agents to clearly see what he was doing. Seated in the back of the cab, he waited to give the driver directions until he saw the two agents also hail a cab.

"Columbus Circle," he instructed the driver.

The uptown ride to the monument took about fifteen minutes. The crosstown traffic was surprisingly light for the time of day, and the driver made exceptionally good time. He pulled to the curb as near the circle as he could. John paid the fare and got out. He saw the second cab stopped a short distance away; a moment later the two agents were standing on the sidewalk.

John walked toward Central Park, entering the south end not far from 59th street. The number of people in the park was minimal. It was early in the morning on a work day in Manhattan. Taking one of the paved foot paths, he walked toward the center of the park, being careful not to be obvious, while surreptitiously observing his companions.

When he came to a spot where two of the paved paths intersected, he quickly ducked behind one of the large maple trees lining the path. He didn't have to wait long before his two followers came to the same spot.

John jumped out from behind the tree, gun in hand. He took the man by the back of his neck, squeezing hard enough to immobilize the agent, who grimaced in pain as John's fingers dug into his nerve centers. The gun was pointed directly at the forehead of the female agent.

"Move," he commanded. "Off the path, into the trees. If either of you reach for your gun, I'll kill you both before you can take your next step."

The woman followed his directions, as he forced the man in the same direction. They reached a grove of trees fifty yards off the pathway. The trees completely obscured their presence from anyone walking by.

"Stop right here," he ordered.

Chapter Eight

The woman stopped and turned to face him. John released the man, pushing him toward his partner. Both instinctively raised their arms in the air. John kept his gun pointed directly at the two.

"Okay, put your arms down. I don't have to ask who you two work for because I'm not even sure you know. But I do know that I don't like being followed. I presume you know who I am or at least what I do."

"No, sir," answered the clearly frightened woman.

"That wasn't a question. Just listen to me. You two on my tail is the problem and it's extremely dangerous. Not for me. For you. You leave me with two options. I can kill you both right here, right now. Or you can walk away and deliver a message to your boss. Which is it?"

The two captive agents looked at each other, searching for an answer. Suddenly, the female made a quick move to draw her pistol from its holster. John's normal reflex would have been to shoot her in the chest. Double tap, center mass. Instead, he slapped her across the face with the barrel of his pistol, knocking her to the ground.

"See? Now that was stupid, and it really pissed me off," John said. "I told you not to do that. You're damned lucky you're not dead!"

He pushed the male agent toward his partner. "Help her— and don't reach for your weapon. I'm not in the mood to be gracious a second time."

The agent helped his partner to her feet. He took a white handkerchief from his pocket and pressed it firmly against the cut on her cheek.

"You'll live," John said. "That scar will get you a life-time pension. Now, here's what we're going to do. I'm not going to kill you unless you get stupid again. Believe it or not, we're supposed to be on the same side. We work for the same agency. If I kill you, I'll be a criminal and hunted down. Ain't gonna happen, kids!" he mocked.

"So, what you're going to do is wait right here until I walk away. Then you're going to scream and holler until somebody comes to help you and you get her to a hospital. That will need a couple of stitches. When you talk to your boss, you're going to tell him that the next agent I see following me will be returned in a body bag. And that's the last time I'm going to let this slide. There will be no more warnings.

"Second, you're going to make it clear to him that should I have to do that, I'll be on my way back to D.C. to deliver his own personal body bag—with a big red bow on it."

He waved his weapon in their faces as they looked up at him from the ground. They were angry and defeated, knowing that they had failed and compromised themselves to a far superior agent.

John continued, "Be sure to tell Bruce that I have my assignment well in hand and tell him that I also have Kristin. If he wants to live, and if he wants her to return safely and in one piece, back the fuck off!"

He turned and walked away, sure in his own mind that he had delivered his message loud and clear. Now it was up to others to decide if he would have to kill them or not.

Chapter Eight

From Central Park, he took a cab back to the hotel to retrieve what little was in the room, most importantly, the satchel containing the million and a half dollars. From the hotel, he walked as fast as he could to the designated address on Park Avenue, where he hoped Kristin was waiting. He entered the lobby through the main entrance, fighting the flow of adrenalin and attempting to maintain control of himself. He wanted to look like all the other businessmen prancing around.

He heard a woman clear her throat from behind a column close to the concession stand. Kristin! He took her by the hand and led her out through the lobby's rear entrance, practically dragging her south to 42nd street, where he hailed a cab, directing the driver to take them to Penn Station.

He didn't say a word to Kristin, fearing what the driver might hear. When they reached the terminal, John purchased two tickets for a northbound train that would take them up the Hudson Valley to Albany.

Only after they had walked down to the lower track level did he find a secluded spot where he could fill her in on the events that took place after they separated. Luckily, their train wasn't due for another thirty minutes, giving Kristin enough time to absorb what he told her and to calm herself.

After boarding the train, they sat back and enjoyed the scenery as they escaped the confinement of the big city and entered the rural valley through Westchester County and Duchess County, passing by the United States Military Academy at West Point, perched on the opposite side of the river.

Instead of staying on the train all the way to Albany, John abruptly grabbed their bags and exited the train in Beacon. There, he rented a car from Avis, drove across the river to Newburgh, and turned north on Route 9W.

"Where are we going?" Kristin asked for the tenth time.

"Somewhere where I can be sure you'll be safe," was all he would say.

They drove north on 9W through Middle Hope, Marlboro, Milton, and Highland, all towns John knew from his childhood. When they reached Kingston, they crossed the bridge over the New York State Thruway and again turned north, this time on Route 32.

"Why not take the interstate, John?"

"Toll booths."

"Toll booths? What do you mean? I think you have enough cash in that bag to pay a toll."

"The Thruway is a toll road, and all toll booths have cameras. We don't need our picture taken."

An hour and a half later John navigated his way around Albany, finally reaching Route 4, which ran north, tracing the historic river. They drove through Cohoes, Half Moon and Mechanicville, past the Saratoga National Battlefield, Schuylerville, Fort Edward, Queensbury, and into Fort Ann, where he turned west on Route 149.

Kristin was mesmerized by the change of scenery along their route. From the narrow streets and tall buildings of New York City to the rolling hills of the lower Hudson

Valley, then the Catskill Mountains off to the west, and now, the foothills of the Adirondacks. From gray concrete to lush green, sprinkled with lakes of blue and black, the river narrowing as they progressed north.

"Hungry?" said John.

"Thought you'd never ask."

He drove a couple of miles farther and pulled into a parking lot full of pickups and ATV's. A small neon sign with only the letters R-E-S-T blinked a welcome.

"What is this place?"

"The best and cheapest food within a thousand miles," John said. "I promise you won't be disappointed."

When they walked in, all heads turned to see who was entering. Some eyes fell on Kristin because of her good looks. Others fell on John. A chunky woman who appeared to Kristin to be in her late fifties walked up to John and lacing her arms around his neck, planted a big juicy kiss on his cheek.

"Hey, stranger. Where the hell have you been?"

John returned both the hug and the kiss, lifting the woman off the ground as he did so. "Hey, Gretch. Been traveling. What's the special today?"

"Good food, good company... and lots of me. Who's your friend?"

"Gretch, this is Mary. Mary, this is the true love of my life and the owner of this fine establishment, Gretchen Black."

Gretchen stuck out her hand in a warm welcome. "Pleased to meet you, Mary. Hope this pain in the ass is treating you better than he treats the rest of his friends around here. Come on Matt, your favorite table is waiting for you."

She led them toward the rear of the dining area to a table for four butted up against the back wall. Two other customers reached out and took John's hand as he passed, greeting an old friend returning home. Kristin was silent the whole time, trying to sort through what was going on around her.

"Matt?" Kristin whispered, as they followed Gretchen to their table.

"For the sake of the crowd," John whispered.

"Here you go, you two. What'll ya have, late breakfast or early lunch or both?"

"I'll have your famous Reuben sandwich, fries, home-made baked beans, and a slice of cherry pie," John rattled off.

"You got it! And how about you, young lady?"

"I don't have a clue. I just got here."

"How about I order for you?" Gretchen suggested.

"Great! I'll trust your judgment."

John looked up at Gretchen. "How's my place doing?"

"Doing fine. I was there day before yesterday. Cleaned it up a bit and brought in a couple of sacks of groceries just like you asked. Should be good for a couple of weeks."

Their tone and the volume of their conversation was far softer and lower than the greeting at the door. Their facial expressions were far more businesslike, now that they were not being studied by every other customer in the restaurant.

"Great!" he answered. "Need a special favor. I'll be leaving tomorrow or the day after. Mary will be staying in the cabin by herself. I'd appreciate it if you would sort of look after her while I'm gone."

"Be happy to. How about I stop by this evening and we can talk some more?"

"Sounds good. See you then."

As she walked off to place their order, Kristin looked across the table at John. "What's going on?" she asked. "Who is this lady?"

"I've known Gretchen most of my life. She's very special. I'll explain more later."

Chapter Nine

After finishing their meal, they each gave Gretchen a hug and started for the door. John exchanged greetings with three or four of the local men sitting at other tables enjoying their lunch. It was clear that he was a fixture of the area and knew many of the local residents.

They got into the rental car and drove a couple of miles along the highway before turning right onto Buttermilk Falls Road. After a mile or two, the road changed from pavement to dirt as it weaved its way through the southern edge of the great northern forest of Upstate New York. Fifteen miles into the wilderness, a yellow pipe extending across the road blocked any further travel.

"Where are we?" Kristin asked. They both had been silent on the ride along the rough dirt track. She had tightly gripped the door handle during the rough ride, distracted only by the natural beauty enveloping the roadway as John drove them deeper into the forest.

"We're just about home."

He got out of the car and walked to the yellow pipe, where he opened what she recognized as a call box. It contained what looked like a military field telephone. John lifted it, waited a few seconds, spoke into it, and then returned to the car. A few minutes later, a man appeared on an ATV. He dismounted and removed a big padlock that secured one end of the metal pipe to a steel post anchored to a large block of cement buried in the ground.

"Where the hell are we!" Kristin asked again.

John drove through the gate, followed closely by the ATV. Less than a mile further, they drove into a settled area surrounded by very large homes nestled into the hillside and overlooking a large body of water. Kristin was amazed at what she saw. Each house was clearly worth over a million dollars.

They drove by nearly a dozen houses before passing through the main part of the developed area. A couple of hundred yards later, John pulled up in front of a moderate-sized log cabin. Big, but tiny in comparison to the homes closer to the entrance. There was nothing beyond this point that Kristin could see except for a steep hill at the rear of the cabin.

"Welcome to my place," John said. "Come on in and let's get you settled a bit."

Kristin explored the interior with her eyes. It was warm but bright, decorated in earthy tones and overstuffed furniture. She walked around, taking in everything, and found two bedrooms. Each had its own bathroom, and there was another full bath in the hallway. There was a well-designed kitchen. She could also see a loft area that looked like it offered additional bedrooms.

"Whoa! I'm impressed. Who lives here? Whose place is this?"

"It's mine, and I live here whenever I can."

"Wow! Very nice. Manly, but not obnoxious. I like it. I mean, I really like it!"

"Good, because you're going to be here for a while. Bob, the gentleman on the ATV who unlocked the gate, will watch over you, and Gretchen will be sure you have everything you need."

"Who are these people?"

"Kristin, all you need to know is that I trust them both with my life. I have known them for many years. They are the only people in the world who know who I am and what I do. They will protect me—and you—at the expense of their own lives. You'll get to know them a little better in the coming days. But please promise me you won't grill them. They won't answer any questions, and you will only put distance between you and them if you insist on probing. Just accept that they are close to me—very close."

"Okay, but where are we?"

"This is part of what was once a very large estate belonging to an early twentieth century industrial mogul. At one time, he owned miles and miles of land on this side of the lake you saw on the way in. When he died, he willed most of the land to the State of New York, keeping only enough area to give each of his kids and a few very close friends enough space to build their summer homes."

"How did you get here?"

"I'm a distant relative of one of his old friends. This cabin was once the caretaker's home. Bob is the current caretaker and he lives in a house close to the gate. He and I served together in the military. He is as gentle and soft as a horse's nose, but as deadly as a rattlesnake."

"And Gretchen?"

"Gretch and I go way back. She was a close friend of my mother. She took care of me when I was a little boy—even changed my diapers. After my mom and dad died in a plane accident, she was like a second mother to me."

"And these two people know what you do?"

"Yes, and they help me when I need them. They are a vital part of my team. Bob covers my butt when I need it, and Gretchen mends me when I need mending."

"Okay," Kristin continued. "Now that we're here, what do we do?"

"You'll stay here, where you'll be safe. Bob will make sure of it. I can leave you here without worrying about your buddy Bruce finding you."

"But all those people at the restaurant? They knew you."

"No. They know the guy who lives here. They know the guy who travels selling chemicals and who hunts and hikes in this area. Many of them are hunting buddies. That's all they know of me. They accept me as one of their own. That's why I know it's safe to leave you here."

"What about you?"

"I'm going to Canada."

"Canada? Why the hell are you going to Canada?"

"Kristin, we agree that this whole thing stinks. The mission itself. Calling me in out of the field. The amount of money involved. The two of us being followed. Then me being followed. Then you again on the train and in New York City. The whole string of events from the moment you told me to come in. It stinks and I've got to find out why. The best way I know how to do that is to get right into the middle of it."

"So what are you going to do? Go to Canada, give the prime minister a jingle on the phone and say, 'Hey, I've been hired to kill you, but first how about we have lunch?'"

"Something like that. I have an old contact in Canada. She's the daughter of a very big client of mine. A chemical client from my cover job. She worked for her father before going into politics. He's a very powerful man in Canada. He helped launch her career, and he donated a lot of money to the prime minister's campaign.

"Before that, we did lots of chemical deals together for her father's business. She did all the buying for him. They bought millions of dollars of stuff from me over the years. We became friends, or at least as close to friends as I was allowed with anyone. And now she's the Minister of the Interior for the Canadian government. I'm going contact her and see if I can learn anything."

"I saw her on the news when she visited D.C. "She's strikingly beautiful. Exactly how close were you two?"

Chapter Nine

"Fear not, my love. She's a great person, and I think a lot of her. However, she would be far more interested in you than she would ever be in me. She's openly gay and has a full-time companion, much to the chagrin of her father. I think there was a time when he looked at me as a potential son-in-law. But she finally came out to him when she was in her late twenties."

"Good! Um...I mean, okay. So, it sounds like you have a good idea and a plan coming together. When do we leave?"

"Not *we*—me! If I go, it has to be a solo trip. I want to keep a very low profile and get in and out as quickly and as quietly as possible. I need to think this through a bit more before I finalize going up there or not. Two of us crossing the border will require two sets of false documents and I'm not prepared for that right now.

"If I go, I'll leave tomorrow or certainly within the next couple of days. I want to let your two buddies in D.C. cool off a little. That will give me some time to think this through. And besides, I need some rest and some good home cooking. I know my way around a kitchen pretty well."

"Really!" she said in delight.

"Yep! So, let me see what Gretchen stocked in and I'll get started on dinner. You make yourself at home. In the morning, we'll hit the discount mall a few miles from where we turned off the highway and buy you some clothes. Oh— I usually call the bedroom on the right home. There are a couple more upstairs if you like those better. Take your pick."

Kristin picked up her bag and headed toward the bedrooms. As she approached the two on the lower level, she took a slight turn to the right. John took note but did not comment or react to her entering his bedroom. Instead, he began rummaging through the pantry to see what groceries Gretchen had stocked up on. He had alerted both Bob and her from a burner phone, messaging them that he might be in the area soon and would have a guest with him.

He found everything he needed and began preparing what he hoped would be a surprise for Kristin. He wanted to impress her. Dinner would be an all Italian extravaganza starting with pasta, followed by chicken parmesan with roasted potatoes, stuffed mushrooms, and a broccoli salad, all capped off with chocolate tapioca pudding with roasted coconut topping and whipped cream—lots of whipped cream—and a cherry.

He worked for hours while she sat on the overstuffed couch watching the latest news. As the clock approached six, he joined her, carrying a small tray with two glasses and a bottle of Italian Chianti.

"It's a great red wine, and I promise it will go great with dinner."

"If you don't feed me soon, I'm going to melt away from the fantastic aroma you've produced all afternoon."

"Okay, then let's eat."

Chapter Ten

It was closing in on nine o'clock by the time they had polished off the bottle of wine that went so well with the Italian food, washed the dishes, and cleared the kitchen. After the last fork was put back in the flatware drawer, they turned to each other and took a deep breath, each far more exhausted then either had realized.

"I'm pooped," Kristin said, as she leaned back against the kitchen counter.

"Me too," John added. "What do you say we call it a day and hit the sack."

"I'm with you. Day's over."

"I'd like to take a shower before we go to bed."

"Good idea, me too," Kristin agreed.

John went directly from the shower to the bed and crawled in between the crisp clean sheets that waited so invitingly. Kristin followed a few minutes later. Both were naked, but the events of the day overpowered any physical desire either might have had for the other. They embraced each other without a word and within minutes were sound asleep in each other's arms, lulled by the comfort, silence, and peace of their surroundings. They felt safe.

John awoke shortly before daybreak, slipped into a robe, and made a large pot of coffee. Mug in hand, he went to his desk and pulled out a map of New York. He knew the roads throughout the area very well, but wanted to confirm in his own mind the route he would take if he decided to go Ottawa.

The fastest route would be via I-87 south to Albany, then I-90 west to Syracuse, picking up I-81 north to the Thousand Islands bridge, where he could cross the border and proceed to Ottawa.

However, I-90, the New York State Thruway, was a toll road. Toll roads have toll booths with cameras, and having his picture taken is not something that a man in his profession enjoys.

So, he plotted an alternate route, one that would take a couple of hours longer, but had no cameras. No cameras, no pictures fed to any arm of law enforcement, state or federal, that might have an interest in his whereabouts.

Kristin joined him shortly after 7:30. He made them a breakfast of egg, cheese, and ham on a bagel, fresh orange juice, and hot coffee. Gretchen had supplied them well. He would have to thank her with a big hug and maybe a box of chocolates.

Chapter Ten

"I see you've been studying the map. Have you decided to go?" Kristin asked.

"No! The whole thing is rattling around in my head. Getting in and out of Canada without raising any flags is only part of the problem. I've also got to be very sure of how to approach the situation once I get there. The last thing I need is to expose myself to the Canadian authorities and have *two* countries after my ass."

"All I've ever heard is how porous the border with Canada is and how easy it is to cross over."

"Yeah, well that might have been true a few years ago when all you needed was a smile. But then 9/11 came along. There are still places where a person could very easily sneak across the border on foot and sort of melt into the population. That's not what works for me. I need a car when I cross, so that means I must drive over the border.

"But, first things first. We've got to get you to the outlets down by Lake George for some fresh clothes and whatever else you need. Then I need to talk with Bob and Gretchen to let them know how long I expect to be away. I'll ask Gretch to stay here at the cabin with you if you want."

"Why would I want that?"

"Well, it's a strange place and you'll be all alone. Thought you would like some company."

"I think I'd like to stay here alone if you decide to go. If that's okay?"

"It's fine. I'll leave you her number, so if you change your mind or need anything, all you have to do is give her a call and she'll come running. Bob will be close by, and he'll keep an eye on things."

"When can we go shopping?"

"Right now. Stores open at ten. I need to talk with Bob for a minute and then we can leave. Takes about half an hour to get there."

"What do you need with Bob?"

"I want him to follow us and check our tail. See if anyone is onto us."

Fifteen minutes later, they were on their way. Bob had already left. They drove back to the paved road and then onto the highway. John turned right, driving west toward the Adirondacks. About five miles from where they got on Route 149, John saw Bob ease his car out from behind an old country gas station across from a convenience store. He knew he would stay a quarter of a mile behind them to be sure that no unwanted company was on their tail.

They turned left on Route 9 and were immediately at the outlets. John shepherded Kristin through the stores, where she hesitantly bought enough clothing, underwear, and toiletries to last at least a couple of weeks. She hesitated with each purchase until John insisted by taking the items she showed interest in out of her hands and carrying them to the register.

"John, I can't afford all of this," she protested.

"I can."

Chapter Ten

Thirty minutes after they entered the first store, John's cell rang. He took it out of his pocket, looked at it without answering, then slipped it back in his pocket.

"Bob?"

"Yep. All's clear. Keep shopping."

By the time she insisted that enough was enough, it was time for lunch. They got back in the car and drove a few miles south into the town of Queensbury. He entered the parking lot of a national restaurant chain and parked.

"Aren't you taking a bit of a chance being spotted bouncing around out here?" Kristin asked.

"Yeah, I am, but it's on purpose. I need to know if anyone has picked up our trail before I head for Canada. Bob is covering us, and he'll spot anyone or anything that looks questionable. The only way I'll know is if I risk the exposure. If someone is on us, I'll know what I have to do next."

"Okay, makes sense to me. Let's eat. Spending all your money has made me hungry."

His phone rang again, a glance again confirmed the all clear from Bob.

After lunch, John drove back to the cabin by a different route. He drove past Buttermilk Falls Road toward the village of Fort Ann. As he drove, he glanced in his rear-view mirror and watched Bob turn left onto Buttermilk. When he reached the village of Fort Ann, he made a couple of quick turns until he found his way to the beginning of Hog Town Road.

"Hang on; this will be quite a ride," he instructed Kristin, who was riding in total silence, trying to figure out exactly what was going on.

After ten miles of rapidly climbing along a narrow, winding, dirt road, they came to an intersection where John turned right.

"I recognize this!" Kristin exclaimed.

"Good. We'll be back in the cabin in ten minutes." He glanced at his rearview mirror.

"What are you looking for?"

"Bob."

He continued until he approached a pull-off at a trail-head a couple of miles from the gate. He waited. Five minutes. Ten. Fifteen. Then he saw a plume of dust coming toward him. Bob pulled up next to John's car, rolled down his window and said, "I'll open the gate."

That was all John needed. He knew they were clean. No one had picked up their trail. They were safe, at least for the moment.

After reaching the compound, John had a brief conversation with Bob out of earshot of Kristin, then loaded himself up with all the shopping bags and led the way back into his cabin. Once inside, Kristin fiddled around putting all her new goodies away while John sat at his desk once again reviewing his map.

When she was done, she came up behind John and gently placed her hands on his shoulders. She bent forward, tenderly kissing the top of his head, as she wrapped her arms around his chest. He took her hands in his and acknowledged her kiss with a soft purr. Both could sense the bond between them strengthening with each moment they were together.

"Thank you, John, for all the things you bought me today."

"I loved every minute of it," he answered.

Kristin accepted his words with warmth and satisfaction. She saw the road ahead leading toward a life together. He saw the same road, but with danger lurking around each curve.

"What's next?" she asked.

"How about a hike up Buck Mountain, followed by a grilled steak dinner and a bottle of wine?"

"Sound like a plan!"

The climb to the top of Buck Mountain was a vigorous hour-and-a-half effort that followed a twisting narrow trail through the hardwood forests of the lower Adirondacks. Kristin was enthralled by the views, the fragrance of the foliage, and the size of the boulders she hiked up, over, and around. When they reached the top of the mountain, she stopped dead in her tracks.

"Oh my God! Oh my God, John. This is spectacular!"

Below her, stretched out to the north and south for over thirty miles, lay Lake George, the dark waters dotted with islands scattered from one side to the other, the entire lake surrounded by mountains embraced in a tapestry of threads of uncountable shades of green from viridian to chartreuse to almost black. The water sparkled like a huge bowl of rhinestones. The mountains seemed to sway to and fro in the light breeze that brushed the leaves of maples, oaks, ash, and beech, the needles of spruce and pines. This was not the work of man.

"Can this be New York?" she asked marveling at the scene before her.

"Yes!" John exclaimed.

"I never would have known this existed. The New York I know is all buildings and taxi cabs and traffic and noise and fumes. This! This is unbelievable!"

"Don't beat yourself up. A few years ago, I brought a friend up here for a day hike. He had lived in New York City his entire life and never been to this part of the state. He had no idea this was right in his backyard. He was just as astounded as you are. Most of the world thinks New York stops at the northern tip of Manhattan."

He let her soak up the beauty, let her absorb and be absorbed by the sights, the sounds, the fragrance, and the textures surrounding them. He smiled at the look of amazement on her face as she took in the world around her. His world!

"Look over that way." John pointed northeast. "See that little area of water way off in the distance? That's the southern end of Lake Champlain. A little over a hundred miles up the lake is the Canadian border. About thirty miles in that same direction is Fort Ticonderoga and a little beyond that is another fort at Crown Point. New York State is on one side of the lake and Vermont on the other. This is an area loaded with American history."

Turning to the northwest, he pointed toward the mountains on the other side of the lake. "If you drive in that direction, you will have to go over a hundred miles before you reach the St. Lawrence River Valley. In these mountains, I can lose my body, while finding my spirit in the same instant.

"I love it here. I love everything about it, even the cold, snowy winters. When the lakes are frozen over and the mountains covered in snow, it becomes a winter wonderland. I love to sit in the forest just as a new snowfall begins and hear nothing but quiet. It's so quiet you can hear the snowflakes floating through the air.

"I have sat in these woods for hours and watched deer and wild turkeys and squirrels and coyotes and all sorts of other creatures walk so close to me that I could reach out and touch them. I love it in the fall, when all you hear is the rustle of leaves or the rain of beech nuts falling, finding their way to the ground.

"This is where I come from. This is where I come to find peace. This is where I come to heal."

"John, I had no idea all of this was here. Promise me you'll show me more. All of it. Please promise!"

"I promise."

They sat together on top of a house-sized rock admiring the visual feast that Mother Nature had spread before them. For almost an hour, neither spoke a word. They held hands in silence, letting the mountain breezes cleanse them.

Finally, Kristin broke the silence with a question. "What is that white building across the lake?"

"That's the Sagamore Hotel. It's an early-1900s resort, originally a retreat for the rich and famous. Still very popular. Great place to spend a couple of days treating yourself to wonderful food and the spa, to spoil and pamper yourself. It's a throwback to the spa resorts that were the playgrounds of the industrial giants of the early 1900s.

"Not too far south of here is the town of Saratoga Springs, where people came for the healing qualities of the mineral waters that bubble up out of the ground. And it was where many came a hundred years ago to sit outside in rocking chairs during the winter to allow the cold, clean air to cure their tuberculosis."

"Can we go there? Can we spoil ourselves for a few days there too?"

"When this is all over, I'll take you there for a long weekend."

"Promise?"

"Promise!"

Chapter Eleven

That evening they grilled steaks on the deck over-looking Lake George and enjoyed each other's company along with a bottle of vintage red wine. Afterward, they curled up on the couch in front of the fire. Even at this time of year, the nights were cool enough to enjoy the warmth of an open fire.

"Mind if I turn on the TV for a little? I need to get an update on the news," John said.

"No, go ahead," Kristin replied. "I'm going to freshen up before we go to bed."

"Okay," he replied as he turned on the TV with the appropriate remote control. He watched Fox News for fifteen minutes, then switched to CNN, then to MSNBC to see what each was reporting. None of the stations was reporting anything of interest or related in any way to issues that might affect his mission or the relations between Canada and the United States.

All he heard were the usual politically-motivated comments on one side trying to discredit the other, neither side making any headway, while preaching to an audience that wasn't listening and didn't care. The normal day-to-day pissing contest between the two forces inhabiting the I-495 loop around Washington that no one would ever win.

After thirty minutes, he headed for the bedroom. Kristin was already in bed, looking through a magazine when he slipped in beside her. Without saying a word, he took the magazine from her and let it slip to the floor. They looked at each other in silence, letting their eyes speak far more clearly than any spoken word possibly could.

They made love to each other tenderly and gently and lovingly. There was a sense of finality and urgency in their touch, each knowing that tomorrow opened the door to an ugly world, so different from that which surrounded them on this magical day.

John slipped out of bed at 5:45 in the morning. He went quietly to the kitchen and started a pot of coffee. When it was ready, he poured himself a mug and went out on the deck to watch the sun's first rays kiss the tops of the mountains across the lake.

He was thinking, planning the days ahead. What he did and the level of success he had would determine the course of his life—and Kristin's—forever. He was at a juncture he had never encountered before. He had to choose blind loyalty to those who had controlled his life for years, or he had to question these same people to determine what the motive was behind the orders he had been given.

He had never before doubted. He had never before felt that he had any reason to doubt. But this was different.

Something didn't fit right. His brain struggled for clarity. *Do I blindly follow my orders no matter what... or do I stick my neck out? Do I play the good soldier, or...?*

He sat, drinking his hot coffee as the rising sun began to light his way to the answers he needed. Kristin came out and sat beside him in silence. She knew he was struggling. She reached to take his hand, to let him know she was there if he needed her.

After a while, she asked him a telling question. One that charted the course he had decided upon. "You're going to Canada, aren't you?"

He answered her question with a question. "Kristin, do you remember from your history classes in school what the Nazi officers of World War II used as a defense at their war crimes trials?"

"Not sure what you are asking, John."

"The German officers, the heads of armies, the elite of their country, the intelligent leaders, all stood and tried to justify what they had done, the killing of six million Jews in the camps and the slaughter of the Russian people. They all used the same excuse. They were just following orders. They justified everything they did and tried to get away with it by saying that they were just following orders from their superiors."

"You're going to Canada."

"Yes," he finally answered.

"Then what?"

"Once I do, I will be sealing my fate. Whether I'm right or whether I'm wrong about all of this, I'm done. I will have betrayed people at the highest ranks in our government. I will be considered a traitor. Either way, I will be exposing a plot that could lead to an international crisis.

"I'll have to disappear, go on the run. That alone doesn't concern me. I've lived in the shadows most of my life. I have tons of money stashed away, so how I support myself isn't an issue. But surviving is. For the first time, I will become the target, the hunted instead of the hunter.

"I know what's at risk, what the consequences are, but I can't just blindly accept this mission. I can't accept killing the leader of another country, one of our closest friends and allies for some trumped-up reason. It makes no sense. It doesn't even sound real to me."

He turned to her and looked directly into her eyes. "You have a decision to make. You can go back to D.C. today. I'll put you on a plane in Albany. You can tell them that I kidnapped you. Forced you to come with me, and then you talked me into letting you go.

"They won't believe you, but they won't do anything. It might take awhile, but you'll be okay. Your career will be over. They'll fire you in a month or two, say your performance sucks or something like that, but you'll survive.

"If you stay with me, you will have to live the same life that I do…on the run. Looking over your shoulder at every turn. Questioning everyone you meet, every pair of eyes that look at you. It's not a fun life Kristin. Not at all."

Chapter Eleven

Her eyes never left his. She listened, taking in every word he said, studying every nuanced expression on his face. She examined his soul through his eyes.

"Isn't there any other way?" she asked.

He paused, looking off across the mirrored surface of the lake. "I don't know how. I've got to think. I need some time to concentrate and try to figure some things out. But, now, no, I don't see another way."

When he stopped talking, she was quiet. Finally, she asked him one question. "Do you love me, John?"

"More than I can admit, even to myself," he whispered. "It's what's making this so difficult."

"Then you have your answer. I stay with you. I stay with you, John. And you'll find a way. I know you'll find a way for us to have a life together."

They embraced, their strength and conviction cementing the bond that had formed between them. They were one. They held each other for a long time until Kristin stood and walked back into the cabin. Tears filled her eyes.

John heard her walk to the bedroom to take her morning shower. He sat on the deck looking out over the lake. It gave him peace. He picked up his map again, studying the route he would take to Canada.

It would be easy to avoid the toll roads and the toll booths with their cameras. The border crossing was another problem. All crossings photographed the vehicle, the driver, and the license plate. The passports of everyone inside of the vehicle were scanned for verification.

Most people leaving the United States anticipated dealing with U.S. customs agents at the border. He knew this was not the case. When leaving the U.S., the customs agents a citizen had to deal with were those of the country they were about to enter, not the one they were leaving. John knew that it was the Canadian customs agents whom he would have to deal with when he crossed the border. He wouldn't have to worry about the U.S. agents until he attempted a return.

Although it seemed that he had neutralized Bruce and his people, he still expected that an alert had been issued to all law enforcement agencies to keep an eye out for the two of them and report back to Washington. He would bet that was especially the case at the Canadian crossings.

On second thought, would Bruce risk alerting the Canadian agents? An alert to the U.S. agents would not raise any flags. But, alerting the Canadians? That was another matter altogether. They would ask questions and expect answers. They didn't work for Washington and didn't blindly take orders from the U.S. government. Alerting them could create another whole set of issues that John felt sure Bruce, and whoever was pulling his strings, didn't want to deal with.

John messaged Bob, asking him to come up to his cabin. He wanted to tell him of his plans and ask him to keep an eye on things, particularly Kristin.

Ten minutes later, Bob was sitting next to him sipping a mug of coffee. "What's up?" he asked John.

"I'll be leaving first thing in the morning. Kristin will be staying here. I need you to keep an eye on her."

"You know I will. Why would you think you need to tell me that?"

"You need to be extra watchful, Bob. It's our own people out for me. I've pissed off the U.S. government this time. That's a new ball game for all of us."

"How long will you be gone?"

"Shouldn't be more than a couple of days. At the outside, maybe three or four."

Bob knew better than to ask anything more. He had been at this for too many years to pry or to expect any further insight as to what John was up to. He accepted that John knew what was best.

John continued. "Drive down and visit with Gretchen and tell her the same thing. Tell her I'd like her to be available to come up and stay with Kristin if need be and to keep the place supplied."

"John, are you getting into something with this woman that we need to know about?" Bob knew he was in uncharted territory asking John these questions. "We have never seen you act like this before. Are you putting yourself at risk because of her?"

John thought about the question. "She's different Bob. She has become very important to me. That's why I'm asking you to be more alert than usual."

"You know I will be, but it's you I'm worried about."

"So am I, old buddy. So am I. This is a different kind of position I find myself in. It could change a lot of things.

But don't worry. You and Gretchen are well taken care of no matter what happens."

"I should punch you right in the friggin' face for saying that or even thinking that was my concern. Neither Gretchen nor I do what we do because of the money you pay us. She would kick you in the balls if she were here right now."

Just then, Kristin came out to the deck. "What's up, boys? I couldn't help hearing some angry words coming from out here."

Bob jumped in. "Our pal here just pissed me off."

She looked at John with a questioning expression. "What's up with you? Can I play referee in this squabble?"

"No need," Bob interjected as he stood to leave. "I'll take care of things while you're gone just like I always do." He talked pointedly at John. "Including this pretty lady of yours. If she's important to you, then she's important to me."

He stomped off toward the kitchen with coffee mug in hand, mumbling under his breath the entire way through the cabin.

"What was that all about?" Kristin asked.

"I said something in the wrong way...or he took it in the wrong way. I'm not sure which. He'll be okay. I'll give him a big hug before I leave and all will be well again."

"You two are too much like brothers to be upset with each other."

"Yeah! We go a long way back and went through a lot together before I got involved with all of this. He *is* like a brother."

"He even looks like you. I'll bet in a crowd, it would be easy to get the two of you mixed up."

"That's happened. We used to play games with the girls we dated. We confused a lot of people by switching our clothes and even our cars when we were in school. We had a lot of fun doing that kind of stuff. Once, I was in his car with a girl and his girlfriend saw me kissing her. She thought it was Bob, out with someone besides her. Took us a month to convince her it was really me."

"Make it better with him John. Please."

"Don't worry, I will. Now, what would you like to do for the rest of the day? How about a walk down by the lake?"

"I saw a canoe yesterday. Can we go for a canoe ride?"

"I have a better idea. How about we pack a couple of sandwiches, paddle out to one of the islands and have lunch sitting on the rocks overlooking the lake?"

"I would love that," she replied as she threw her arms around him and gave him a big kiss. "I would absolutely love that!"

Chapter Twelve

Following an afternoon on the lake, they sat together on the deck and enjoyed some quiet time reading. That evening, they ate a light dinner and went to bed early. They took each other with a warmth and tenderness found only in those who sensed the security and strength of the person they were with. There was no need for words. Words would only get in the way.

Kristin knew that he would be leaving in the morning. John knew that she was worried and wanted to go with him, but couldn't. There was no need to discuss it and beat it to death. Their time together was better spent expressing their love for one another.

He said goodbye at ten o'clock the following morning. She hugged him, fighting back the tears of tension that were welling up inside her. For her, as well as for John, this was a new experience. She loved him and was scared to death that this could be the last time she would ever see him. By this time tomorrow, he could be dead or locked away in a Canadian prison somewhere deep in the Arctic.

Chapter Twelve

He said little in the way of goodbye. His mind was already focused on what lay ahead. He drove to Route 9 near the outlet stores they had visited and turned right, traveling north through the village of Lake George. At the north end of the village where the road split, he bore to the left toward the town of Warrensburg. Passing through this old, historic town, he drove northwest a few miles to Route 28. Bearing toward the west, he continued traveling deeper into Adirondack State Park and higher into the aging mountains.

A few miles later he came to a bridge that crossed the rapids of the Hudson. Here in the mountains, the Hudson was a wild, untamed river that bore no resemblance to the wide, flat expanse of water most knew as it neared New York City and the Atlantic Ocean. Here, close to its headwaters, it was a whitewater river littered with rocks and boulders.

Next came the town of North River and the hamlet of North Creek. The highway climbed a long, sloping hill after crossing the railroad tracks that once carried timber and iron ore out of the mountains down to the mills near Glens Falls. Just as he was approaching the top of the hill, he turned to the left onto a stretch of the old highway that paralleled the new road for a mile of two, rejoining it on the other side of the crown of the hill.

When he got to the juncture, he pulled over and parked behind a barrier of low-growing scrub that hid his car from view. There he waited. Five minutes…ten…fifteen. Watching. He then made a U-turn on the old stretch of highway, retracing his route back to where it branched off the new road, where he turned left and proceeded once again, having assured himself that he was not being followed.

In a couple of minutes, he entered the village of Indian Lake, where he stopped to visit one of his favorite old mountain general stores across from the local fire station. He didn't need anything, but it was another way of checking his security while enjoying some old memories of the times he had hunted in the area and purchased supplies and equipment at the store.

After a few minutes, again satisfied he was not being followed, he got back in his car and drove past the junction of Route 30 and on to Blue Mountain Lake and Long Lake and then into the town of Tupper Lake. He pulled over into a roadside diner, where he sat at a table overlooking the lake and the highway.

After eating a sandwich, he returned to his car, picked up Route 3 and drove for a couple more hours, passing through the towns of Cranberry Lake and Star Lake, ultimately coming to Harrisville. There he turned right onto Route 812 toward Gouverneur. An hour and a half later he arrived in the city of Ogdensburg on the Saint Lawrence River.

The twisting and turning trip had taken over six hours, but he was sure that the time was worth it. There were numerous opportunities for him to check if anyone was on his tail. By the time he reached the river city, he was sure that there was zero percent chance that he had been followed.

All along the way, he had to fight to keep himself from being distracted, lost in the beauty of the greens and the blues that painted the hills and lakes surrounding him as he drove through these ancient mountains. Nowhere in the world was there a stronger pull on his soul than here in the Adirondacks. In his mind's eye, he could see the views from atop many of these mountains. Hundreds of lakes of all sizes filled the valleys surrounding the steep slopes, creating the illusion that each mountain was an island floating in a world of lush green and gray rocky cliffs.

He drove a short way north on Route 37 until he came to the international bridge carrying traffic over the mighty St. Lawrence into Canada. He had used this bridge many times in the past. This was one of the more obscure crossings, used mainly by the locals, unlike other crossings scattered between Montreal and Buffalo. Much to his surprise, the approach road to the customs check points were blocked by U.S. border patrol and state police vehicles with red and blue lights flashing wildly.

If the powers in D.C. didn't want to directly alert the Canadian customs agents to watch for him, all they had to do was block him from ever reaching the crossing gates. And that's exactly what was happening. He counted at least a dozen law enforcement vehicles blocking every lane of the entry with agents and police searching every vehicle that approached the crossing. Some carried rifles and others had tethered dogs ready to spring into action upon command.

He felt reasonably sure that his false identity documents would get him past the Canadian customs agents, but he was unsure he could get past the gauntlet spread out across the roadway in front of him. Now was not the time to test the proficiency of any of the agencies represented by all the flashing lights. He would have to find another way across the river.

A couple of miles south of the bridge, he pulled into a small strip mall to park and think through his next step. He got out of his car and walked around a bit to stretch his legs after the long drive through the mountains. Darkness was approaching.

He went into a convenience store to buy a bottle of water. There were no other customers in the store. He approached the register to pay for the water. The attendant was distracted by the latest copy of *People*. She never looked up from the pictures of the "100 Most Beautiful People."

"That'll be a dollar twenty-nine," she said, extending her hand.

John placed the cash in her hand and asked, "Is there a good place close by to get some supper?"

"Depends on what you call good."

"Something more than fast food."

"About a mile south of here there's the Riverside Inn. Good steaks and better than average Italian food," the top of her head said. John couldn't tell what color her eyes were or if she even had eyes. They never left the article about the beautiful people.

"Thanks," John said and left the store without any concern that he would ever be identified as having been there. He could have been naked and left the same impression.

He drove south and in a couple of minutes he saw a sign on the right side of the road announcing the Riverside Inn. Beneath the title, he read "Nightly Dinner Cruise." He parked and entered the large dining room overlooking the river. To his left was the reception desk for those looking for a room at the inn. To his right there were about a dozen tables spread out awaiting the evening's customers. Right now, there were only two couples seated at tables awaiting their meals. It was still a bit early.

An attractive middle-aged woman approached him. "Good evening sir. Are you joining us for dinner?"

"Yes."

"Will anyone be joining you?"

"No. I'm alone. Could you please seat me overlooking the river?"

"Certainly. Please follow me." She led him to a table for two overlooking the water barrier that lay between him and his desired destination. "Malcolm will be serving you this evening. He will be with you in a moment."

"Thank you," John replied and took his seat. Moments later a young man in his very early twenties approached the table and introduced himself while placing a menu in front of John.

"Good evening, sir. My name is Malcolm, and I will be taking care of you this evening. Can I get you anything from the bar?"

"How about a club soda with a lime twist. Lots of ice please."

"Yes, sir," Malcolm replied as he turned and left the table.

John looked out over the water thinking about his objective and how he would get into Canada without challenging the customs agents or the state police or any other agency represented by the personnel blocking the bridge crossing.

While waiting for Malcolm to return, he noticed a small group of people gathering on the dock under a sign announcing that the dinner cruise boarded in less than half an hour. Malcolm reappeared carrying a single glass of club soda with lots of ice.

"Malcolm, tell me about the dinner cruise."

"Well, sir, it leaves in about a half hour. The boat cruises up the river for about thirty minutes, passing under the big bridge. Then it crosses over to Canada for a brief stop at a waterfront bar owned by the same people who own this place. After enjoying a brief stop and hopefully a drink at the bar, the customers reboard the boat and cruise back in this direction for about an hour, during which time dinner is served."

John suddenly realized what the young man was telling him. He saw a solution to his problem unfolding right in front of him.

"Do you know if there are any openings for this evening?"

"I'm certain there are, sir. At this time of year, we hardly ever have a full complement of customers."

"Can you check for me please and if there is an opening, would you please add me to the roster. The name is Harrison, Samuel Harrison."

"Certainly, Mr. Harrison. Let me go check. You will be required to have a passport before boarding."

"Not a problem. I have it in my car."

John waited patiently. In less than five minutes, Malcolm returned.

"Mr. Harrison, I'm pleased to tell you that there are plenty of openings on the cruise boat for you to join them this evening, and I've placed your name on the reservation list. You should probably head down to the dock within the next few minutes to join the group."

"Thank you, Malcolm," John said as he placed a twenty-dollar bill in the young man's hand. "This is for your great service. Thank you again."

"Yes, sir. Thank you, sir," Malcolm said as he looked down at the money in his hand. "Please come back and join us for dinner another night."

John withdrew his passport from his overnight bag and walked slowly down to the dock. He paid the receptionist for his reservation, flashed his passport, and boarded the boat. All the other customers seemed make up two groups dining together. He was the only person on the boat not attached to one or the other of the groups. Recognizing this, he quietly faded into a corner of the rear deck and stood by himself observing the others as they enjoyed their time together.

Soon after boarding, the crew untied the mooring lines and pushed the boat away from the dock. The engine rumbled and the boat shook as it began to fight the strong current as they headed downstream toward the bridge.

He pretended to be taking in the sights while cruising the international waterway. No other countries on earth had the kind of relationship that existed between the United States and Canada, one that would permit a group of people to cross their borders unchecked and unquestioned. All this was working to John's immediate advantage.

Twenty minutes after leaving the dock, the boat passed beneath the Ogdensburg Bridge and slowly worked its way across the river. Ten minutes later, it approached another dock above which hung a sign announcing the River Inn Two in both English and French.

Once the boat was tied up to the dock, all the passengers stepped off and headed directly to the dockside bar overlooking the river. John followed the second group, but instead of turning right toward the bar, he continued toward the front door of the building under a small neon sign flashing *EXIT.* No one challenged him in any way. He was in Canada.

Chapter Thirteen

John walked slowly and steadily through the front door of the establishment and across the parking lot. Ascending the slight grade of the driveway, he came to Route 2, running parallel to the St. Lawrence. It was approaching eight o'clock. He mentally ran through his mind the next steps in his process of getting to Ottawa.

First, he needed transportation. With no major airport or town anywhere nearby, renting a car would be a problem at this hour of the night. Besides, even if he arrived in Ottawa tonight, it would be far too late to accomplish anything or to even contact anyone he might want to talk with.

So, he set his first objective to finding a place to spend the night. Looking left and right along Route 2, he saw a 1950-ish motel sign flashing within walking distance of the restaurant.

He entered the office and asked the lone attendant if there were any rooms available.

"Sure thing, mate. Not exactly a high demand in this area," came the reply from an obvious Australian import.

"Can you tell me where I might be able to rent a car?"

"Yeeah," came the heavily accented reply. "Place neah heah in Johnstown. But they're closed now. Won't open again until 6:30 or 7:00 in the morning. They'll bring the car right to your door just like advertised on TV. Theah telephone numba is listed in the brochure in your room."

"Thanks!" John paid for the room with a single large U.S. currency bill. He took the key to the room assigned to him and walked out of the office area.

After entering the room, he sat on the bed holding a burner cell phone in his hand, wanting to call Kristin just to hear her voice. But he couldn't...wouldn't. Instead he undressed and showered before crawling into the U-shaped mattress and curling up thinking of her. It didn't take long before he fell asleep with her image gracing his dreams.

By 8:00 a.m., he'd had two cups of coffee with a large cinnamon roll and had signed for a rental car using yet another fake driver's license and credit card. Mr. Harold Johnson was now on his way to Ottawa. By 10:00 a.m., he had arrived in the capitol, secured a room at the Marriott, a short distance from the Canadian Parliament building, and walked to the seat of the nation's government.

It was a magnificent building built of reddish brown sandstone on the precipice overlooking the Ottawa River. The building was in the Province of Ontario. Across the river lay the City of Hull in the rebellious French separatist Province of Quebec. Little did John know that he would be discussing this very topic in just a short time.

Chapter Thirteen

He joined a tour group with an English-speaking guide in a large tent set up outside and to the left of the capitol. The guide led the group through the main floor of the building, providing peeks into the two main chambers where the ministers from around the country met to debate the issues confronting this very complex country.

Like the United States, Canada's sheer size and diversity of peoples was impressive. The population included Native Americans, French Loyalists, English settlers. Add to that the huge immigration of peoples from Asia. From the big cities of the east and west to the smallest of towns in the Arctic, every issue was pulled in multiple directions.

The tour reached deepest into the capitol near the fabulous octagonal wood-paneled library with its vaulted ceiling. John let the tour group drift off while he pretended to be studying a portrait of a long-dead king of England. When he was alone, he reached for his cell phone and dialed a number on his contact list.

"Office of the Interior," the female voice answered and immediately repeated the salutation in French.

"Good morning. Is the minister available please?"

"May I ask who's calling?"

"My name is John Anderson. I'm an old friend of the minister's. I'm here on an unexpected visit and would like to say hello if she's available."

"Oh yes, Mr. Anderson. I remember you. I worked for the minister and her father on their ranch. I remember your visiting them many times. I'm sure she would love to speak with you. One moment while I check with her. Hold on, please."

The phone went silent for a couple of minutes.

"John, where are you?" a cheerful voice leaped from the phone.

"I'm here in the capitol building. Near the library."

"Don't move. I'll be there in five minutes."

In four minutes, Minister of the Interior Emily Brown appeared in the hallway, racing toward him with a big, broad smile radiating across her face. She threw her arms around John and gave him a huge kiss and a hug that nearly took his breath away. He returned both, lifting her off the floor and spinning her around like he did when she was a little girl.

"How long has it been?" she asked.

"Since you became famous and important?"

"Oh hush. I'm neither. It's all my father's fault I'm here." She stepped away and looked at him. "You look wonderful. What brings you to Canada?"

"And you look absolutely beautiful. Your new position must be agreeing with you. How is uh…"

"She's fine. We have a house here in town and we're doing well. Daddy has come around and accepted her fully. The last couple of years have been great. And you? Has some poor unsuspecting woman latched onto you yet?"

Chapter Thirteen

"Actually, there is someone. She has become very important to me in a very short time."

"Tell me about her."

"Emily, before we do that, there's something we need to talk about." His face clearly reflected a very serious image.

"What's up, John?"

"Where can we talk? We need to be private and secure."

Emily's expression took on a somber look as John's words impacted her. She took him by the hand. "Come with me. I have just the place and it's right around the corner."

She led him to the entrance of the library. Once inside, she took him into a small reading room tucked underneath the circular balcony surrounding the interior of the most beautiful room John had ever seen in any public building anywhere.

Once inside, she closed the door and sat down at the small table against the back wall of the room. John sat at the other end.

"Okay, John. What's up?"

"Em, I do other things than sell chemicals. I have another...profession that I'm involved with."

"Hold on, John. I know more than you might think. When my dad was hoping that you and I might become a couple, he had you 'checked out,' shall we say. We know you have a clandestine position with your government."

"There's more to it than that, Em. I um—I sort of take care of the enemies of the U.S. in a rather...final fashion."

She looked at him with a blank expression on her face.

"In a final fashion? What exactly does that m—? Oh no, John! You don't—?"

"Yes, I'm afraid I do."

"Oh my God! That answers a lot of questions. That's why you always seemed to be in the same country where something...someone..."

"Yeah, now you're getting the picture."

"Oh my God, John. Am I in danger? Is my father? Have you come here to—?"

"No, no, no! That's not why I'm here. No way I could or would ever hurt you or your father. You both mean too much to me. I could never do that."

"Then, what? I'm struggling with this whole idea of your being a— a hit man, for Christ sakes. My God, John!"

"I need to discuss with you the mission I've been given. I can't believe it, and I'm having a very difficult time accepting it," John confessed. "I'm putting myself...my trust in you and myself at great risk just being here. I've never questioned any assignment given to me. I've been paid a huge amount of money to...to—"

"To *what*?"

"To kill your prime minister!"

Chapter Thirteen

"What?!" Shock dominated Emily's face and body as she sprang to her feet. "What did you say? Are you joking? You were sent here to assassinate our prime minister?"

"Not exactly. I wasn't sent here. It is supposed to happen when he visits New York City for the conference at the U.N. I came here on my own to get to the bottom of this. I told you, I have serious doubts and concerns about this assignment."

"I would think so!" she exclaimed. "We're your closest ally and you're been ordered to kill the head of our government? I can't believe what I'm hearing."

"Please calm down, Emily. That's why I'm here. I can't believe it either. There must be a reason, but I can't imagine what it might be. Do you have any idea what might be happening that could come close to justifying such an order?"

"John, I'm flabbergasted. I'm flabbergasted about the whole thing. You and your role. This unbelievable idea."

"Emily, please. I know this comes as a shock and surprise. But I need your help. I need you to stay focused."

"Surprise? That's putting it mildly, to say the least. More like shocked and stunned. Bewildered might come a tiny bit closer to my state of mind right now."

"I understand, Emily. But the question is, how do I get to the bottom of all of this? How do I find out why I've been given this outlandish mission?"

She paced the tiny room, pondering his question. She repeatedly glanced at the man she thought she knew. The man, if her father had had his way, might have ended up being her husband. Finally, her face brightened. She regained her composure.

"The only way I know is to ask him."

"Ask who?"

"The prime minister."

"What?"

"You heard me. If someone wanted to kill him, I would think that he would have some idea who it was and why."

"But—"

"No buts, John. You came to me for help, and that's the way I see it. I'll give him a call and tell him we want to meet with him."

Now it was John's turn to react in surprise. "You can get the prime minister's attention that quickly?"

"He and I go a long way back. He knows I know things about him. He responds whenever I need him. Besides, do you have a better time?" She reached into her pocket, withdrew her cell phone, and dialed a number followed by a three-digit code tapped into the keypad. Within seconds she was connected.

"Is he in?" was all she said. "Peter, it's Emily. I need to see you immediately. No, no. Nothing like that. This is extremely urgent and equally important." There was a pause. "No, not in your office. I think this needs to appear to be more casual and unofficial. Can you come down to the library? I have someone with me you must meet." Another pause. "Yes Peter, it means right now. I can't overemphasize the importance." Pause. "Okay, ten minutes then."

· They waited in silence. Emily paced the room, looking at John in disbelief, trying to absorb what she had learned about him in the last hour. He had transformed from potential husband to government assassin. An enemy to her country and to her. He knew what was processing through her mind, and he decided to let it go without any further explanation.

Ten minutes later, Prime Minister Peter DuBois burst into the room. He was not a big man. He was about five foot ten and weighed around 180 pounds. But what he lacked in physical size, he more than made up for in energy and personality. He was one of those people who made you look for the electrical cord running from his butt to a wall socket to keep him charged up. He gave Emily a modest hug and turned to John, extending his hand in greeting.

"I'm Peter DuBois," he said. "It's a pleasure meeting you."

"Maybe not," Emily said. "Please, Peter, sit down. We have something very alarming to discuss."

"Okay," Prime Minister DuBois answered, reading the grim expression on his long-time friend's face.

"Peter, this is John," Emily began, quite obviously not adding a last name. "I've known John for 15, maybe 18, years. He has been a supplier to my father's ranch and businesses for many years. That's how he and I met. He has something he needs to tell you."

"Okay," Peter said. "But why so grim? It can't be all that bad."

"Yes, it can," Emily replied. "Go ahead, John."

The prime minister turned to face John with an expectant look. John took a moment to collect himself before speaking. He finally decided to come right out with it and get it on the table.

"Mr. Prime Minister, I've been assigned to kill you!"

Peter DuBois jerked upright in his chair, looking startled at the stranger sitting less than five feet from him. He glanced back and forth between John and Emily. John continued.

"I am a highly trained agent of the U.S. government, and my latest assignment, presented to me just a few days ago, is to assassinate you when you visit New York City to deliver a speech at the U.N. I'm having a great deal of difficulty accepting this assignment and thought I'd better get to the bottom of it. So, here I am."

"Wow! You're serious?"

"Deadly!"

"Holy—! Should I call security?" Looking at Emily, he asked, "Should I have this man arrested?" He turned back to John. "Who ordered you to do this?"

"It came down through my control officer. I was called in from the field for a meeting with her superiors. I asked them the same question. I can't tell you exactly who signed the order, if there is an actual signed order. But I can tell you that it came from very high up."

"How high?"

"The very top."

"You mean the president?" Emily asked.

"I don't know for sure. But, yes. I think it came from the Oval Office."

"But why?"

"That's why I'm here, Emily. I don't know why, and I can't blindly accept this assignment the way I'm supposed to. This whole thing has been extremely out of order. There have been things that have taken place before and since the meeting that make me very uneasy. I won't get into the details of what has taken place. Just accept that people in my line of work get very nervous when someone is looking over their shoulder. Very nervous. And when things happen that make us nervous, we often end up dead."

"So you came here to cover your ass?" the Prime Minister asked.

"No, sir. I came here to find out why the president of my country would have reason to kill the prime minister of Canada. By coming here, I certainly wouldn't be covering my ass. I'm exposing myself to you and to your government, and I'm violating my position with my government. I don't see that as covering my ass.

"I have tried to come up with some plausible reason for this assignment and I can't find one." He turned to Emily. "Em, I told you there was someone important in my life. She is my control officer. I have her hidden safely away for now. She too is at a total loss with this assignment. She too has put her career and her life on the line because we both think this stinks to high heaven.

"When the mission was revealed to me— that was the first time she heard of it. That alone alerted us that something wasn't right. We were both startled at what we were hearing.

"I have never questioned an assignment before. I've always carried out my mission without exception. But this one is different. It makes no sense to me whatsoever. I'm not a robot. I have a brain and my brain is telling me that there is something far more sinister behind this than I can figure out."

Peter DuBois laced his hands together and leaned his chin on his fists, his eyes focused on an invisible target buried somewhere within the small table separating him from his would-be killer. After what seemed like an eternity, he looked at his friend and subordinate.

"Emily, you might want to leave the room right now. If you stay, you are going to hear some things that you will never be able to repeat or discuss and that could very well make you the next target for this man or his replacement. Your choice. I'm good whether you stay or decide to step out."

"I'll stay," she replied without hesitation. "I've known both of you for most of my adult life, and if there is any way that I can help get to the bottom of this, I'm here for you both."

"Okay," the PM replied as he turned to John. "Okay, John with no last name, here goes. Very few people know what I'm about to tell you but, given what I expect your expertise is, you won't have any problem verifying what I'm about to say. I should give you some history so you will understand what I believe the reason is for your being given this 'assignment,' as you call it.

"The first place I wanted to go to college was in the U.S. I applied and was accepted at Duke University in North Carolina. I wanted to follow in my father's footsteps in the medical field. It was my dream school and suddenly, there I was. A seventeen-year old Canadian kid totally out of his element in this beautiful school in the United States of America. I had to pinch myself about a dozen times a day to realize that I was actually there. My head was swimming.

"When I first arrived, I walked the campus over and over, admiring the ivy-covered buildings, the massive chapel, and one of the world's most famous medical facilities. I was mesmerized by the place.

"I was assigned a dorm room and met my roommate. His name was— Roger Adams."

"What?" Emily exclaimed. "*The* Roger Adams? The man who is now the President of the United States?"

"Yes. *That* Roger Adams." He answered her, but his eyes never left John's. They were locked into one another digesting, measuring, weighing every word.

For the next hour, Peter DuBois slowly and carefully, doing his best not to skip anything, even the smallest detail that he thought might be relevant to his story, told John and Emily how, shortly after arriving on campus, he met a girl. Her name was Grace. Her father was an Irish immigrant who had worked hard and was very successful in the hardware business, owning a dozen stores throughout the Southwest.

Her mother was a full-blooded Navajo. She was a talented artisan well known in the New Mexico and Arizona art markets and quite successful in her own right.

Grace had her mother's jet-black hair and high cheek bones and her father's bright blue eyes. She was beautiful, as well as extremely intelligent.

They fell in love. They were inseparable, spending every available minute together. Two kids head over heels for each other. They would run off to the beach on weekends and walk the Outer Banks for hours on end.

There was only one problem in their relationship. Roger Adams. He too fell in love with Grace. He kept his distance because of the relationship with his roommate. But his passion for her grew with each passing month.

One day, shortly after returning from the holiday break, she went to their dorm room looking for Peter. He wasn't there, but Roger was. Alone with her, he made a strong play for her, which she immediately rejected. He grabbed her and tried to kiss her. She pushed him away and ran from the room and found Peter. She told him what had happened. The incident dealt a damaging blow to the relationship between the two men.

Roger denied that he had made any such advances toward Grace, in essence calling her a liar. The relationship between the two roommates became increasingly tense until early in February when once again, Grace went to the dorm to meet Peter.

He had been delayed by his professor and arrived about ten minutes late to find Grace lying face down on the floor, dead. There was blood all over the floor around her head and more blood on the footboard of Roger's bed. Roger was nowhere to be found.

The police found Roger about 30 minutes later, bent over a book in the campus library. Both men were brought in for questioning. Every other resident of the dorm was also questioned. Peter's alibi held up; he was with his professor at the time of Grace's death.

Roger's alibi was ultimately accepted as well, since there was no evidence to prove otherwise. However, the police and others accepted it with a considerable amount of reluctance.

In the end, the death was ruled an accident. The official cause was that Grace entered the room, caught her foot in a small scatter rug in the middle of the room and fell backward, striking her head on the footboard. She was killed instantly.

Peter was devastated. He confronted Roger, who immediately and angrily denied having anything to do with Grace's death. But, there were too many unprovable coincidences that kept Peter from believing him. Peter believed that Roger was responsible for her death. End of story.

"He killed her!"

Chapter Fourteen

"What!" exclaimed Emily and John in unison.

"You're accusing the president of the United States of killing your former girlfriend? You're accusing him of being a murderer?" John said in amazement.

"I'm sure of it," Peter DuBois replied.

"Holy shit!" John exclaimed. "Excuse my language, but…"

The prime minister calmly resumed. "I believe Grace went to our room looking for me and found him there alone. He tried to make another advance toward her and she refused. He pushed her, or she tried to get away from him and she fell, hitting her head. When I confronted him, I knew immediately by the expression on his face that he was lying. He killed her. In my heart and in my head, I'm one hundred percent sure of it, and he knows that I know it. As sure as the three of us are now in this room, I'm positive he killed her."

Chapter Fourteen

"But why didn't we hear anything about this during his campaign? Why didn't the press blast this all over the front page?" John asked.

"For two reasons. First, his father, the former senator, was a powerful man when we were in college. I'm sure he covered up the whole thing with a few well-placed telephone calls to the right people in law enforcement and the media.

"Secondly, your president is, and will always be, the media's darling. They wouldn't or couldn't bring themselves to tell the truth even if they knew what it was. From the time he was a high school star basketball player to this very day, in the eyes of the media, he could do no wrong. He is media-made.

"I left Duke almost immediately after I returned from Grace's funeral and came home to Canada. It took me a long time to get over her death. I didn't return to school for almost two years. When I finally did, I stayed here in Canada.

It was my parents who finally got me straightened out. I never saw or spoke to Roger again, not even to this day when we are the heads of our two respective governments and our countries the strongest allies in the world."

"But why would he want to have you killed?" Emily asked.

"The death of Grace was not the only incident Roger was involved in at Duke."

"Wait a minute," John jumped in. "He didn't graduate from Duke. During his campaign, he made a big deal about graduating from a very liberal west coast school. What happened?"

"You're right. After the incident involving Grace, he had another run-in with a female student who reported him to the school administration. She accused him of attempted rape. She later dropped the charges. The police subsequently found out that Roger's father had negotiated a substantial cash payment to cover the cost of her education.

"To keep it quiet, the school asked Roger to withdraw and nothing more would be said about it. That's when he transferred to that liberal west coast school he brags about.

"While he was there, he had at least two or three more run-ins with the school's administration and the police, all concerning sexual misconduct with female students. His father finally took the bull by the horns and placed him in therapy.

"He was confined to his parents' home for almost a year, along with two full-time therapists. When everyone concerned considered the therapy successful, he returned to school as if nothing had happened. And because all the therapy took place at home, there is no public record of any of it.

"Nothing was ever said or recorded concerning all of this. Even the names of the two therapists have evaporated into the great unknown of the Adams' bank accounts. The only problem Roger has is me.

"He knows that I know the entire story. He knows that I had others watching him and providing me with every bit of information I could get my hands on. He knows that

I have all the details, all the dirt. He knows that I kept tabs on him the entire time. He knows that I have never forgotten or forgiven."

"But you've never said a word to anyone about any of this?" John asked.

"No. I see no need to drag up the past. What purpose would it serve? It would appear as if I, the prime minister of Canada, representing the Canadian government and people of this nation, had a personal grudge against the president of the United States and therefore your entire country. It would get me and Canada nowhere. Keep in mind, there are no public records to support what I'm telling you and the Adams fortune would be spent to the last dime to destroy me and my story."

Emily and John remained silent for several minutes, letting Peter DuBois' story sink in.

"I still don't get it," said John. "It's been so many years and you haven't exposed him. Why would he take such a drastic step at this point in time?"

DuBois looked thoughtful, then continued, "There's more. I believe he is unbalanced. I have sources in your government who would agree with me. His actions are irrational and those around him have had to take control more than once. I firmly believe that he is psychotic, and that it stems back to the events in our college days—the death of Grace and the secret therapy he went through at home. I believe that Roger Adams is a paranoid schizophrenic.

"I think that he wants to create a reason to take control of all the ports of entry along the U.S.–Canadian border from Quebec to the Great Lakes. To do that, he needs to create a crisis in Canada that would indicate an unstable enough condition to take military action to protect the flow of shipping traffic along the Saint Lawrence River corridor. And now that you are here telling me your story John, I believe he sees my death as the means to two ends, getting me out of his life and creating the crisis he needs."

"You have got to be kidding! You can't be serious about this!" Emily said.

"Quite! I'm only speculating. However, in his mind I think I am still a threat to him and that this plot conveniently provided him with a way of killing two birds with one stone. I only wish I knew which was the driving force. I wish I knew if getting me out of the way was an excuse to take over the ports or if it was the other way around."

"Wow! That's way out there. But I can see the logic in it. Do you know where I live, I mean, my real home?"

"No," Peter responded. "I know nothing about you, John."

"I live in the upper Hudson Valley of New York. Some years ago, I read a book called *Saratoga* by Richard Ketchum. It's a history of the entire New York–New England–Canada area from the early settlement days through the American Revolution. It portrays the importance of the water routes of the St. Lawrence River, Lake Champlain, Lake George, and the Hudson River for trade and military control of the entire region. What you're saying is like reliving that book in modern times."

DuBois continued, "In addition, Roger knows that I was a member of the Provincial Government of Quebec.

He knows that, as unlikely as it might be, French Quebec would still like to break away from the rest of English-speaking Canada. The port of Quebec City would be the first port along the trade route. And, he knows if Quebec were to succeed, I would be asked to return there as the prime minister of the new country of Quebec."

"This gets better and better! Next you'll tell me that you have proof he's an alien from another planet."

"Well, he did go to school in California."

"Point well taken," John said.

"Now what?" Emily asked.

Once again, they sat in silence until John spoke up.

"Two things, Mr. Prime Minister. First, you're going to become ill. Too ill to attend the U.N. conference in New York. I've been ordered to make your death appear as if it were an accident or from natural causes. If I can't get to you, I can't complete my assignment. So keep your plans to go to New York and to deliver your speech, but then get too sick to attend any of the other events.

Second, you're going to find a way of getting me back into the U.S. tonight without going through the U.S. border check stations. I'm going to Washington. There's something very wrong down there. Adams can't possibly think this is going to work. If he does, he really is delusional. Such an act would be an enormous abuse of power, to say nothing about being unconstitutional. And sick!"

"How do you think he even got it this far?" asked DuBois. "He didn't give you the assignment himself. He had others communicate it to you. He followed some sort of chain of command. So there must be others who know what's going on."

"Well, he has to have some sort of leverage over the people who are carrying out his orders. They also know that it's illegal. One thing I have come to realize is that he intends to pin your death squarely on me. With only a moderate struggle, I got them to agree to pay me fifty million dollars to carry out this assignment."

"Fifty million dollars!?"

"Yep, and I got it up front. There's more to the story that I won't bother getting into right now. However, I'm beginning to think that I'm the well-paid goat in this whole scheme. In the end, neither the president nor anyone else in Washington can in anyway seem to be remotely involved with your death. That's becoming more and more clear to me. But, who and why is someone in authority over me, agreeing to the whole plot? As I've said, something stinks. And I don't want that stink to end up being my dead body rotting away in some landfill. Something stinks really bad and I've got to get to the bottom of it.

"And there's one more thing. I have to figure out a way for me and a very special woman to survive this."

Chapter Fifteen

It wasn't difficult for the Canadian authorities to get John back into the U.S. They drove him back to the Ogdensburg Bridge. Once there, they walked to the Canadian entry side of the roadway. He was then escorted into one of the border crossing huts and he simply walked through and crossed the border back into New York and the good old U.S. of A.

From the duty-free shop near the bridge, he called for a taxi to take him back to the Riverside Inn. He found his car waiting right where he had parked it the day before. It was nearly dark by the time he got on the road. He knew it would be a long drive back to Lake George.

It was risky driving through the mountains on dark and narrow two-lane roads this late at night, particularly as tired as he was. He didn't want to risk hitting a deer or a black bear that decided to cross the road right in front of him. So he decided to take a different route around the mountains. It would also be easier and quicker.

He knew he would never be able to sleep with his head spinning after this meeting, so he decided that he would drive straight through, getting home in the wee hours of the morning.

He sent a text message on his phone. *Bob, I'm six hours out. Will let myself in with second key. Is it in the same location? Please tell Kristin I'll be crawling in during the night.*

A few minutes later, he received two replies: *yes* and *okay*. There was a hidden key near the estate entrance and Bob would let Kristin know he was on his way back. Neither Bob nor John wanted to run the risk of her being startled in the middle of the night. Getting shot as he drove into the compound or opening the cabin door unannounced wouldn't be a good end to the day.

It was a long drive, interrupted only by one gas and restroom stop. He began to tire as he approached the city of Amsterdam, only to be startled back to full awareness by two deer standing in the middle of the road. He had to swerve to avoid hitting them, a very common occurrence along these roads even though he had taken the safer route home. This was still wild country.

The close call, however, served him well. It spiked his adrenaline for the rest of the drive. He decided to stop at a Stewart's 24-hour convenience store near Galway to buy a bottle of water. He drank most of it and splashed the rest in his face to refresh himself. It also gave him a chance to foil anyone's attempt to follow him.

A little over an hour later, he pulled up to the barrier guarding the entrance to the estate nestled on the shore of Lake George. He retrieved the hidden key and unlocked the heavy-duty padlock. Once he drove his car beyond the barrier, he replaced the padlock and key and proceeded to his cabin.

There was a light on, welcoming him with its warm glow. When he stepped into the cabin, he was attacked by a flying woman. Kristin launched herself from across the room, landing against his chest. She wrapped her arms around his neck and her legs around his waist, knocking them both to the floor.

"Oh God, I've missed you," she said. "I've been so worried."

"I'm starved!" he said as she smothered him with kisses.

"I am too. We'll eat later."

She got to her feet, pulled him up, and practically dragged him into the bedroom. By the time they reached the bed, they were naked. They fell onto the mattress and took each other without another word passing between them. Their urgent lovemaking told all that needed to be said.

Exhausted, they lay for a few minutes trying to catch their breath. Kristin would not release her grip on John. Her legs remained wrapped around him, with her arms encircling his neck and chest. Feeling fully exposed, John finally spoke.

"Now can I get something to eat? I haven't had any food for almost twenty-four hours."

"Do you have to get up to eat?"

"Not if there's someone else here who can go into the kitchen and bring me some food."

"Okay!" she said as she released him from her four-limb body lock.

After eating an oversized chicken sandwich made from Kristin's leftover dinner, they returned to the bed and sat facing each other in their robes. Kristin hesitantly asked a question that revealed the newest elephant in the room.

"How did it go in Canada?"

"Well, I was able to contact my friend, Emily. I told her what was going on and naturally, she had a hard time believing any of it. It took me awhile to convince her, but it finally sank in and she accepted it. She picked up her telephone and called the prime minister's office. Within fifteen minutes, he joined the two of us."

"Whoa! She must have some real punch inside the government to get him there."

"I told you her father is a powerful man. Anyway, the prime minister listened to everything I had to say. And then he proceeded to tell me a fascinating story about him and the president. Things I had never heard and I seriously doubt that many other people in the world have ever heard. We have a potential motive to kill the PM."

"What did you come up with? Why would President Adams want to kill him?"

"Hang on to your hat. You're not going to believe this."

Chapter Fifteen

They talked for over an hour while John relayed the entire meeting and all the information, new and old, and the nuances of his meeting in Canada. Kristin silently absorbed every word. She asked several questions to help clarify this stunning story to get it clear in her mind.

Once John had finished talking, they leaned back against the headboard processing the last forty-eight hours. It was approaching four in the morning when they finally slid down beneath the bed covers and fell asleep in each other's arms.

Kristin woke to the smell of fresh coffee. She found John sitting in his usual chair on the deck, gazing off across the lake. It was a chilly morning as many were this far north, no matter the time of year. She approached from behind him, lacing her arms around his neck and shoulders and kissing him gently on the cheek. He reached back and caressed her soft, smooth face.

"You'd better put some clothes on. I asked Bob to join us this morning. I want to bounce my meeting in Canada around among the three of us. I need as much input on this one as I can get."

"Bob knows what you do?"

"Yes. He was also a candidate for a job like mine. He was injured quite badly during the training and couldn't continue. That's when he and I came to the arrangement we have now."

"And Gretchen?"

"No, she was with me long before that. I think I told you that I've known her since I was a kid. She knew Bob and his family as well. She knows enough, but doesn't want to know the details. She knows that I can come home pretty beaten up, both physically and otherwise. She's like a mother who only wants to know what her children do after they've done it. She doesn't want to know ahead of time. It would drive her nuts. Here comes Bob."

Kristin quickly dashed into the cabin, returning moments later wrapped in her favorite plush terry cloth robe.

"Morning, you two," Bob said as he climbed the stairs up to the deck. "I heard you come in early this morning. Everything okay?"

"Yeah. It was a long trip. I put the key back where you left it."

"I know. I checked."

"Thought you might."

"So, what's on the agenda this morning?"

"I've got to kick my trip around with you guys. The meeting I had in Canada was a crazy one, and I need input from you both."

John brought Bob up to speed. However, this time, for Bob's sake, he started at the very beginning when he got the call from Kristin to come in for a meeting.

He disclosed the assignment he was given and the meeting that took place with Bruce and Andrew. He repeated everything his old friend, Emily, as well as the

Prime Minister had to say and most importantly, the story the PM told him about the President of the United States.

John gave them as much detail as he could recall, trying not to confuse the actual story with all that was swirling around in his head since he started the lonely drive back to Lake George. It was sometimes difficult for him to separate the story from the speculation.

When he was finished, he went into the kitchen, returned with a pot of coffee, and refilled everyone's mug. No one spoke. The only sounds came from the surrounding woods and critters near the lake.

"Well, what do you think?" John asked at last.

"I'm having a hard time digesting this," Bob said.

"Me too!" added Kristin.

"Welcome to my world," John said.

"How in the world did President Adams keep all of this a secret? How in the hell did the press not dig up all this years ago?" Kristin asked.

"Money!" John answered. "Money and power. Money *is* power. His father had both. His whole family had both. Don't forget, his father was a high-ranking Senator at the time and his mother was very well connected inside the Beltway. I'm sure his father paid off every professor, every college administrator, every doctor, nurse, janitor, news reporter, garbage collector, and dogcatcher who got anywhere near this whole mess.

"There's another factor in play here too. The press reports only what the press wants to report. Roger Adams is a creation of the press. He is and has been their darling since forever. Either they don't know any of this or they choose not to report it. Either way, it comes out the same. So, what do I do now? That's the question."

"Well, I don't see how you can carry out your assignment," Bob began.

"I totally agree," Kristin added.

"If I don't, you both know what will happen. I become a loose end. I will become the target for another agent. The guys pulling the strings behind this can't leave any ends dangling. That's why I'm sure that I'm the goat in this, even if I were to pull it off."

"But if you already believe that you will be eliminated, then not completing your assignment really doesn't change anything," Bob commented.

"Right!" John agreed.

"Yeah! And I can almost guarantee that I know who it is who would be sent after you," Kristin said. "After all, that is what I do. I run agents, and the one I've got in mind is good. Not as good as you, John. But I wouldn't want to go up against him."

The three of them talked for most of the morning, kicking around their thoughts and reactions as well as suggestions. As lunchtime approached, it was clear that there was no real solution or plan that they were going to come up with. The conversation among the three of them flooded John with information for him to take into consideration. Some good, some not so good. That's what he needed to help him come up with a plan.

"There's only one thing for me to do at this point," John said.

"What's that?" Kristin jumped in.

"I've got to deal with this head on. I've got to get to the bottom of this and find out who's behind this whole thing. Who's pulling the strings and issuing the orders. To do that, I've got to go to Washington."

Chapter Sixteen

"I'm going with you," Kristin blurted out.

"Actually, I think that's a good idea. You know your way around D.C. far better than I do. Having you there will be a big help."

"What do you plan on doing while you're there?" Bob asked.

"Plan? I wouldn't say I had a plan now Bob. All I know is that I've got to figure this thing out. And I have an idea how I can at least begin to get a handle on it."

The following morning, Bob drove Kristin and John to the Amtrak station in Rensselaer, directly across the Hudson River from the state capitol of Albany. Both wore western style straw hats to cover their faces as much as possible. Even traveling on a commuter train exposed them to security cameras.

By mid-morning, they arrived at Penn Station in New York, where John purchased two tickets on the express train to D.C. Three hours later, they were at Union Station. With hats tipped forward, they walked through the station out into a rainy afternoon in Washington.

From the back seat of a taxi, Kristin gave the driver the address to her apartment.

"When you get a block away from the address, I want you to slow down, but do not stop," John instructed the driver, a plump, fiftyish gray-haired woman. "I want you to drive by the address nice and slow. Got it?"

"Yeah, I got it. Are you guys on the lam from the law or something?"

"No, just a jealous husband we're trying to avoid."

"Uh huh, heard that one before. Don't worry. I'll go nice and slow." Fifteen minutes later, she slowed the cab to a crawl. "We're a block away," she informed John. "What do you want me to do?"

"Just keep moving, and then turn left at the end of the block," John instructed.

"Got it!"

She drove by at a snail's pace. Kristin looked directly at the entrance to her apartment building while John examined every car parked within the block. He scrutinized every potential point of observation offered by every building within line of sight to the entrance to Kristin's building.

He nudged Kristin's leg and nodded in the direction of a dark gray sedan parked on the opposite side of the street from her building. Then again, as they approached the front steps, he nudged her again and nodded toward the alleyway about a hundred feet farther up the street.

"Okay driver, let's get out of here… nice and easy. Turn left up ahead like I told you," John said as he reached over the seat and slipped a hundred-dollar bill into her hand.

"Got it! Now where to?"

Kristin directed the driver to a third-rate motel in Capital Heights, just off Pennsylvania Avenue, to the east of the Capitol area.

"Are you sure you want to stay in this part of town?" the driver asked. "It can get pretty rough out this way."

"We're sure," John answered.

Capital Heights was a lower-income section of D.C. made up primarily of minorities of various ethnicities. Not the kind of area John would expect anyone to be looking for them or keeping a watchful eye. It was not an area frequented by tourists. It was a good place to hide.

Once they had checked into the hotel, they sat down to discuss their drive-by of Kristin's apartment.

"What did you see, John?"

"There were at least two cars, each with two agents in them. And there was another agent in the alley using a camera with a telephoto lens to watch your building."

Chapter Sixteen

"Are you surprised that they were there?"

"I would have been much more surprised if they *hadn't* been there."

"Why would they be there?"

"Well, pretty lady, you are a missing federal employee off in parts unknown in the company of a government assassin of whom they are currently unsure. It's the first thing they've done that makes sense."

"Okay, now what do we do now?"

"Our homework!"

For the rest of the afternoon and evening, they worked on John's laptop. They searched for information on the early life of President Adams. Kristin used her codes to access the law enforcement data banks and search for any information concerning the death of a young woman during his early days in college. And they searched for addresses. One in particular.

The following morning John rented a car from an agency that would pick them up at their motel. After checking out of their 'deluxe' room, they drove around the city, checking out the various addresses they had researched. John was looking for people and places that might be of interest to him in finding more information that would justify the mission assigned to him.

At four thirty in the afternoon, Kristin dropped him off near an apartment complex in Alexandria, Virginia. They had purchased two burner phones from a Walmart earlier in the day, one for each of them. They agreed that Kristin would wait in a shopping center parking lot and would stay there until he called for her to come and pick him up. She would wait for as long as it took for him to call.

At five minutes past eight, a man in a suit, carrying a brief case, approached the main entrance to his apartment building. He took the elevator to the eighth floor, inserted a key into the lock on his front door and entered his home. He flicked on the overhead light and froze.

"Hey, Bruce. Welcome home."

"How the hell—?" Kristin's boss said, seeing the man sitting on his couch with a gun in his lap.

"Bruce, come on! Did you forget what I do for a living?" John said. "Come on in and sit down. We have some things to discuss."

Bruce set his briefcase on the floor and sat in an armchair facing John.

"Where's Kristin?" he asked.

"Safe," John answered. "But I'm not sure I can say the same for you or me, Bruce. Unless I get some straight answers to some very troubling questions, you and I are going to have a very unpleasant evening together. Got it?"

Bruce nodded, his eyes locked on John.

"Okay, first question, am I being surveilled?" John asked.

"Yes."

Chapter Sixteen

"By whom?"

"Our agency plus Homeland Security. They have been asked to monitor the borders for you."

"Did they report that I was in Canada?"

"You were in Canada?" Bruce reacted with surprise that he could not hide.

"Yes. Did they report it?"

"No. We had no idea you went to Canada."

"I had a great meeting with Peter DuBois. Very informative."

"You met with the prime minister? How the hell were you able to do that?"

"We'll talk about that later."

"What did you talk about? Does he know about... about...?"

"He does now. Like I said, we had a very informative meeting."

Bruce was obviously stunned by this news.

"Okay," John continued. "So, let's get to it. First, who told your boss to issue the order to kill the prime minister of Canada?"

"It didn't come from my boss."

"What do you mean? Someone else ordered you to assign this mission to me?"

"That's exactly what I mean."

"Who?"

Bruce hesitated.

"Come on, Bruce. Let's not make this more difficult than it should be. I don't want to get blood all over your nice furniture."

Bruce stared at John and then took a deep breath, seemingly resigning himself to the situation in which he found himself.

"The White House Chief of Staff."

"What?" John reacted.

"You heard me correctly."

"William Baxter issued the order? Through whom? Who actually ordered you?"

"He did, directly. He went around and over everyone between him and me. He asked me to meet him for lunch one day about a month ago and led me into this crazy hypothetical conversation about 'what if's,' and after an hour of pure bullshit, he got to the meat of the meeting and finally ordered me to assign you to the job."

"Me or any agent?"

"No, you specifically."

Chapter Sixteen

"How did he even know that I exist? It's not like my name is on a list of 'friendly neighborhood assassins.'"

"I don't know. I was just as surprised as you are when he gave me the order and followed it, giving me your name and ordering you to carry it out."

John was quiet for a moment, trying to sift through what he had just heard.

"Why would you take orders from the Chief of Staff? Why didn't you inform your boss?"

"He leveled some very strong threats at me. Against my career and my family— and my life."

"But, the Chief of Staff! He doesn't have that kind of power or authority in the line of command. Why would you listen to him?"

"He's the Chief of Staff. He speaks for the President. He might not be in the line of command as you understand it, but he is the White House Chief of Staff. He's like a military drill sergeant: he tells you to drop your drawers and take a shit and you answer, 'Yes sir, how high and what color?'"

John paused, then asked, "How about Andrew? How is he involved?"

"He's dead!"

"What?"

"Two days after our meeting with you and Kristin in Baltimore."

"How?" John asked, stunned by the news.

"Hit and run right in front of his house with his two kids not more than five yards away on a street with a twenty-five mile an hour speed limit."

"Damn!"

"That, I'm sure, was a message for me. Someone was telling me that I could be next. They were sending me a signal," Bruce stammered, frightened and shaken.

"Okay, why? Why would Bill Baxter issue such an order? And how in the hell does he believe that he could get away with such an outlandish move? What did he say to you that would or could justify your ordering me to do this?"

Bruce leaned back in his chair and took another deep breath. He seemed to relax just a bit. Some of the tension in the room lessened. The two men sat there having more of a business conversation than a threatening encounter between two adversaries.

"He told me that this had to do with the future of the country. That the president had tried to approach and solve the problem diplomatically for years, going back to when he was a senator, and nothing had worked. He said that Prime Minister DuBois was a stubborn ass and mentally unbalanced. He said that he had issues in his private life that went back to when he was a kid. He told me that DuBois' father had buried everything year after year. He said that the prime minister's policies were endangering our ability to transport goods by way of the St. Lawrence Sea Way ports." Bruce stopped, but obviously was not finished.

Chapter Sixteen

"What else, Bruce?"

"He told me that the prime minister and the president had a long and deeply troubled history and that because of that, they were not capable of communicating successfully."

"Did he tell you what the history was? Why the two men had such a bad relationship?"

Bruce continued. "He didn't say it outright, but he hinted at something about a female. That there was a woman in the middle of it all. He didn't go into any details about the problem or the woman."

"But what he said was enough for you to carry out his instructions? You had to know that this order was illegal and that someone would burn for it. What was strong enough to make you go forward?"

"Well," Bruce began. "He told me that he and the president would see to it that you would be the one who got burned. You would be the one to take the fall. They would see to it that there were leaks at the right time in the right places that would lead the world to you. That you had gone rogue on us and that you were deranged and totally out of our control."

"But you wanted me to make it look like the prime minister died of natural causes. Why would they need to pin that on anyone?"

"That was just a cover. They had every intention of exposing the PM's death as an assassination. Once the Canadian officials announced that it was from natural causes, there would be leaks hinting at an assassination, followed by more and more evidence that it was."

"And?"

"And your name would be included in the leaks. There would be a trail leading directly to you. He assured me that he could support everything he was telling me. He said that all I had to do was check with two people."

"Who?"

"One was his own father and the second was the president's father. He and the president grew up together and their fathers were very close. He said that the two of them were fully aware of the history between the president and the prime minister and that they had it under control years ago."

"His father?"

"Yes. And the prime minister's father as well."

"And the president's father? He told you that the three fathers could confirm the entire history?"

"Yes. They have all been friends for many, many years. Going back to when the boys were in college."

"What?"

"They went to the same college, at least in the beginning. Then the president transferred to another school. But, until then, they lived in the same dorm. Baxter's father was the county sheriff. Bill was a local sports hero in high school. Later his father became a senator and Bill became sheriff. He followed in his father's footsteps, building his own career."

"Holy shit!" John jumped to his feet and very deliberately tromped around the room. "Shit! Shit! Shit!"

"What?" Bruce asked tentatively.

"Shit! Someone is lying. Either you were lied to or the prime minister lied to me."

"What are you saying?"

"Bruce, I got the same story in Canada. Peter DuBois gave me the exact same bullshit, except it was a one-hundred-and-eighty-degree flip."

John repeated DuBois' story for Bruce as close to word for word as he could remember it. He and Bruce continued to discuss the story until both were convinced that it was real and the actors were playing the same roles. The only issue was who was telling the truth and who was lying. By the time they hashed it out, they were both exhausted and sat silently, their minds swirling, trying to unravel the whole mess.

What had become clear to John during his time with Bruce was that the two men were not enemies.

"Bruce, one thing for sure. You and I have got to call a truce. We need to work together. And you have got to get out of here. If you don't, I think you will meet with an untimely death just like Andrew. You won't be around for more than a day of two longer than the prime minister. Once he's gone, you become a very big liability."

"Do you still intend to go through with this assignment?"

"No, but the person or persons pulling the strings don't know that. If they did, both of us would become their prime targets."

"But I don't know what to do," Bruce said. "I'm not like you, I don't have the experience doing what you do. I'm a desk jockey, not a field agent."

"Okay. Here's what you do. First, you are going to get into your computer and retrieve a couple of addresses and telephone numbers for me. Next, you are going call into your office and tell them that you have a family emergency and you have to take some time off." John stopped to think for a moment before he continued. "Where do your parents live?"

"Near Pittsburgh."

"Perfect. The emergency concerns your father's health and you're going to Pittsburgh."

"But they're in Europe on an extended vacation with a travel club they belong to."

"Even better," John said. "Once you've made that call, you're going to pack a bag with some clothes, enough to last you a week or two. No three-piece suits. You won't need them where you're going. Jeans and tee shirts will do nicely.

"Next, I'm going to give you a telephone number. When you call this number, a man named Bob will answer. I want you to say one word and only one word. He will ask you to repeat it twice. After you say it the third time, he will give you an address or a place along with a time. He will meet you there and take you to a safe place.

"Do not, I repeat, do not bring your cell phone or laptop or any other electronic device with you. Bob will scan you before making contact and if he detects any device, he will walk away and leave you there. Got it?"

Another thought suddenly popped into John's mind.

"Bruce, do you have access to my entire file?"

"Yes, of course. You worked for my department long before I was appointed department chief. Your personnel file has been in place since you were first recruited. It's your entire history with the agency."

"And you can access it whenever you want?"

"Yes."

"Can you make it disappear?"

Bruce hesitated. He knew exactly where John was going with his line of questions.

"Yes. I can erase it completely. It would only take one or two key strokes on my computer and you would cease to exist."

The two men looked at each other without speaking. John's eyes said it all. Bruce understood completely.

"You get me out of this mess, and you can consider it done."

"Where are your wife and daughter?" John asked.

"They live in our house in Virginia. This is a rental apartment I keep here so I don't have to travel so much. We keep late hours a lot in our business."

"I want you to call your wife and tell her to be ready to take a trip. Tell her to have her things packed for a two-week vacation and your daughter's things too. And tell her to be sure not to say a word to anyone. Tell her you'll pick her up in an hour. Make sure she understands the gravity of what's happening without really telling her anything. Can you do that? Can you do that without scaring her? Will she go along with that?"

"Yes. She understands my world. She's been dealing with it for a lot of years. She'll understand."

"Good. Tell her you'll be home in an hour."

"But when do I do all of this? When do I leave?"

"Now!"

Chapter Seventeen

While Bruce packed his clothes and toiletries, John placed a call to Kristin, and with a one-word signal, told her to pick him up. A few minutes later, the two men climbed into the rental car. Her jaw dropped when she saw Bruce getting into the back seat.

"Drive!" commanded John.

"But—"

"Drive. I'll explain as we go."

She accelerated away from the curb as John surveyed the surrounding area to see if they were being followed. He hadn't detected any signs of Bruce's building being watched when he'd arrived a few hours earlier. He found the same to be true now. They were clean.

"Where are we going?"

"Philadelphia, by way of BWI."

"What?"

As Kristin drove south on I-495, John filled her in on his meeting with Bruce. She glanced in her rearview mirror several times; Bruce's gaze was fixed, unseeing, on the passing scene, his dazed look becoming more understandable as John talked. When they arrived at BWI and dropped Bruce off at Avis, he and John exchanged a few words that Kristin could not hear. John got back into the car as Bruce entered the rental office.

"Where's he going?" she asked.

"Home!"

For the next two hours they tried to piece together the two stories: the one told by Peter DuBois and the version told to Bruce by the president's Chief of Staff. Where was the truth hidden, and who was giving them the real story?

When they were on the I-695 bypass to the west of Baltimore, John said, "Take the next exit and find us a gas station."

"But we don't need gas yet," she protested, but the look in John's eyes left little room to question his instructions. She took the next exit and pulled up to the pumps at an Exxon Mobil station on the right. They sat at the pumps for a solid twenty minutes, checking every car that drove by, as well as all those parked anywhere nearby. All clear.

As she drove on, she asked, "What did you tell Bruce when we dropped him off at the airport?"

"I instructed him on what he was to do next."

Chapter Seventeen

"And?"

"I instructed him on how he was to contact Bob."

"Contact Bob?" she exclaimed.

"Yes, Bruce and I have struck a deal. I pledged to get him and his family out of this alive."

"In return for?"

"Our future."

She looked at him, obviously puzzled by his explanation.

"I told him not to forget to say the code word, then to wait until Bob asked him to repeat it. And then wait again until Bob asked him for it a third time."

"What is the code word?"

"Ticonderoga. And when Bob asks him to spell it, he has to spell it like this."

John handed her a scrap of paper with the fort's name written out as "Tycondaroga."

"But, that's not the way you spell it."

"Exactly. Bob knows that I can't spell it correctly. If someone does, he'll hang up on them, and they'll never see or hear from him again."

"Clever."

"Clever is why I'm alive. We'll see Bruce in a few days, along with his wife and daughter."

Kristin looked at him, amazed. The more he did for others, the more he put his own life in jeopardy. And here he was, explaining to her that he had just taken his former adversary and his family under his protective wing. The man was a complete contradiction, and that was only a small part of why she found herself more and more in love with him every day.

"You confuse me," she said affectionately.

"Yeah? Join the club."

Then John gave her directions to a section of Philadelphia just north of the Pennsylvania Turnpike extension that connected to the New Jersey Turnpike. He told her to pull into a self-storage facility on highway 309. She punched the code he gave her into the keypad.

"Drive to the end of the first row of units, please."

She did as he asked.

"Okay, park next to that motor home."

In a graveled area at the end of the storage units there were over two dozen RV's of all descriptions awaiting their next road trip. Some had tarps thrown over them. Some had fancy wheel covers protecting their tires. Others were just…waiting.

"What are we doing here?" Kristin asked.

"I want you to meet Ace."

Chapter Seventeen

"Ace? Who is Ace and what is he doing here?"

"Come on, I'll introduce you. Pop the trunk for me and lock the car when you get out."

He took their travel bags out of the trunk. Then he took Kristin by the hand and led her to one of the waiting RV's.

"Kristin, meet Ace!"

"Ace" turned out to be a thirty-five-foot Class A motor home, a beautiful unit majestically waiting to be fired up and taken out on the open road. John reached up under the entry steps and retrieved a key. He inserted it in the door and assisted Kristin up into the motor coach.

"It's…um… beautiful," Kristin said. "But what are we doing here?"

"This, milady, is our temporary home on wheels. With this, we don't have to check into hotels and we can travel inconspicuously."

"Inconspicuously? This thing is a monster. The whole world will see us coming!"

"You're right," John answered. "But they won't see a government agent and a fugitive case officer. They'll see a happy couple cruising down the road on vacation."

"And where would we be going with it?"

"Canada."

"Canada? But won't we have to pass through the border control stations? What about the cameras?"

"No worries. See how high up off the ground we are in this vehicle, and see these huge sun visors across the windshield?"

"Yeah!"

"First, the cameras at the border stations are set to take pictures of passenger vehicles. They're aimed way down low. Second, when we pull down the visors, there is only a narrow slit left for the cameras to catch our image. Now you add a nice big straw hat and sunglasses… Bingo!"

"Okay, I got it. But why do we need to go back to Canada?"

"We're going back to talk with Peter DuBois and my friend, Emily. I'm sure that's where the answers are that I need to hear; I need to hear them from him while I'm looking him in the eye. And I want to get your reaction to him and his story."

"You believe his version of the story, don't you?"

"Yes, I do. I believe him and I think you will too. Plus, I've known Emily for a lot of years, and there's no way she would ever be a part of a lie like this. I'm confident that his is the true story."

"Okay, I'm with you."

"Good. I was sure hoping you would say that. I'd really hate to have to lock you up in this storage unit until I got back."

She gave him an uncertain look.

"Just kidding. I wouldn't lock you up. I'd just shoot you and put you out of your misery," he grinned as he got out of the motor home and walked over to a unit with an overhead door.

He unlocked the unit and pushed the door up, revealing a compact four-wheel-drive white Jeep Renegade. He drove it to the rear of the motor coach and hooked it up to a tow dolly. Then he got back in the coach and climbed behind the wheel. "Here we go," he said, as he started the powerful engine and drove out of the secure facility.

"When will we get there?" Kristin asked.

"Not until midday tomorrow. It's about an eight-hour drive. We'll stop tonight somewhere along I-81 near Syracuse and go the rest of the way in the morning. You're going to love living in this thing and the freedom it gives us. Now, sit back and enjoy the ride."

Kristin did just that. John drove west on I-276 to I-476. Then he turned north and drove through the rolling hills of eastern Pennsylvania until he reached Wilkes-Barre, where the road intersected with I-81. He found a truck stop along the highway to fill his fuel tanks.

"I'm going to park here and get some sleep before we tackle tomorrow. We can use the restrooms inside the truck stop and catch a little sleep right here in the motor home."

The following morning they had a fast-food breakfast before continuing north toward New York. After passing through the Blakely area, it was clear that they were leaving behind the big cities and the dense population of the eastern seaboard. Kristin was quiet, enjoying the beauty of the lush green hills and the scenery of the Poconos and the Catskills. She snuggled into the plush front seat and propped her feet up on the dash, quickly getting accustomed to the comfort of the motor home.

"I have to use the bathroom," she announced.

He pulled the coach to the side of the highway, coming to a complete stop. "Come with me. I'll give you a quick lesson in RV living."

He led her back to the bathroom and instructed her in the use of the onboard toilet. There was enough water in the storage tank to use it, eliminating the need to find a rest area or truck stop.

When she returned to her seat, she said, "I can really get into this way of traveling, John. I love this thing."

"Good. I'm thinking we might be getting a good amount of use out of it in the days ahead." When they reached Binghamton, New York, just across the Pennsylvania line, he asked, "Hungry? We haven't had any real food all day. How about an early dinner?"

"Yeah. I could eat a big steak right about now."

"Me too. I know a place a few miles north of town right along the highway. Easy for us to pull this big rig over and enjoy a good meal before we push on further."

The local steakhouse had a vast menu— if you liked steak. There were fifteen different types of steak on the menu along with two other items, baked potatoes and wedge salad. That was it, the sum total of the menu. Like Henry Ford once said, "You can have any color you want as long as it's black." In this place you could have anything you wanted, as long as it was steak.

"What'll you have?" the waitress asked with a local twang. "We have steak raw, steak rare, steak medium, steak well done and, of course, steak burnt. Take your pick. Comes with baked potato and a salad. You can put ketchup on your potato, but if you dare put it on one of his steaks, the boss will personally come out here and shoot you right between the eyes. What'll it be?"

"I'll have a Delmonico, medium rare...butter only on my potato...bleu cheese on my salad...no ketchup on anything," John said.

"You've been here before, I take it,'" the waitress commented.

John nodded, sharing a big grin with her.

"I'll have the same," Kristin added.

"Good move, honey," said the waitress. When she walked away, John leaned over the table and whispered to Kristin, "Welcome to Upstate New York."

"Well, she *is* sort of... sort of a redneck."

John chuckled at Kristin's observation. "Kristin, the more you travel, the more you'll come to understand that rednecks are not confined to the South. Rednecks live everywhere. Once you get away from the big cities and out where the real people live, you'll find the most down-to-earth people. All they're interested in is living day to day, and they don't give a hoot about impressing the rest of the world. The intellectual snobs call them rednecks. I call them real."

After stuffing herself with one of the best steaks she'd ever eaten, Kristin managed to get back into the motor coach to resume the drive north on I-81. As they approached Syracuse, John spotted a sign advertising a Good Sam's campground near the Onondaga Reservation. He pulled off the highway and followed the signs until the entrance appeared on his left.

"Come with me, Kristin. You need to learn how to do this in case you have to do it when I'm not around."

They entered the office and spoke with the middle-aged woman behind the counter. She had pronounced Native American facial features. Kristin found herself staring at her beauty.

There were spaces available at $45.00 a night. John paid in cash and took the map with the directions to their site, which the woman had outlined with a highlighter. It was a full-service 50 amp pull-through site. Kristin listened to the entire transaction, not understanding anything beyond the $45.00 price.

"Did you understand all of that?" John asked.

"What did you just pay $45.00 for?"

"A campsite."

"Yeah, I got that, but what is a pull-through and full service and 50 amps and all that stuff?"

Chapter Seventeen

John chuckled inwardly, not wanting to embarrass her.

"You are not only beautiful, you are a delight to travel with. "Full service means we have access to water, electric and sewer. The 50 amps is the level of electric service available at the site. There's 30 and 50. A rig this size, with all the stuff it's loaded with, like the big refrigerator and the washer and dryer—it requires 50 amps to operate."

He pointed to another unit already parked. "See how that unit is parked in the site it's on? That's a back-in site. Should be self-explanatory. Now watch what I have to do to park our rig."

He approached the assigned site and simply drove into it and stopped.

"Well, that was easy," said Kristin.

"Yep, this is a pull-through. I didn't have to back it into the space. To exit, I just pull right through. Come outside with me, and I'll show you the rest of the setup process."

They stepped outside, and in just a few minutes he showed her where the various cables and hoses needed to hook up the unit were stored onboard the motor home. Next, he showed her how to connect the electric, water, and sewer services. Then he took her back inside and stood her in front of the coach's electrical control panel.

"Okay, now press that button and watch what happens."

She did as she was instructed and watched one of the four slideouts deploy.

"Wow!" she exclaimed.

"Now press those other three, one at a time."

She did and watched the coach grow larger as each slideout expanded.

"John, this is fantastic! It's huge in here."

Next, he showed her how to turn on the hot water heater and the combination gas/electric refrigerator. She absorbed everything he showed her, fascinated by the whole process and all the features of the motor home.

"Let me give you a tour," John said after they completed the setup. He showed her all the controls, including the hydraulic jacks that he used to level and stabilize the coach. He showed her the entertainment and air conditioning systems, the furnace and the hot water heater, and how the refrigerator worked on both gas and electric.

He led her toward the rear and reintroduced her to the bathroom, finally leading her into the bedroom at the very rear of the coach. She gazed upon the queen-size bed and the closet that stretched the full width of the coach.

"I'm amazed at this thing!" she exclaimed. I've never been in an RV before. This is fantastic. It's like—"

"—a house on wheels."

"Yeah. But I have a question. Where are you going to sleep?"

They both laughed and exchanged a brief hug.

Chapter Seventeen

"This is a midsize unit," John continued. "There are others that are much bigger, with even more features. But I'm glad you like it. We might be in it for a while."

"Why John? Not that I don't like it, but why the sudden switch to traveling in this?"

"Traveling in an RV provides us with a lot of anonymity. You noticed that I paid in cash and that the owner never asked me any questions, not even for an I.D. Try that in a hotel or motel. We can park here for a day, a week, or a month, and no one would give us a second glance. There are nearly twenty thousand campgrounds of all sizes and descriptions in the United States.

"From wherever we're parked, we can go in any direction on any given day. It's a transient life style. We could move from one place to another every day, and no one would be able to trace our movements. The people are always friendly, but never nosy. Are you getting the drift?"

She nodded her head. "You've done this before."

"Yes, many times."

"And the car we are towing?"

"It's hard taking this unit to the grocery store or into the heart of a big city. That's where the Jeep comes in. I can unhook it in five minutes and drive wherever I need to go. It's a four-wheel-drive vehicle, so it's good any time of year in any conditions— snow, rain, mud or sand. The two vehicles do everything I might need them to do. The Jeep provides me with a great deal more flexibility."

"Are you expecting that we might be needing the anonymity and the flexibility?"

"Yes. I asked Bruce if we were being surveilled, and he said that at least two agencies were looking for us. However, they lost us in New York City and haven't been able to pick up our trail since. And surprise! They did not know that I had been in Canada.

"We need to fly as far under the radar as we can for as long as we need to." His mood became more focused and stern. "I've said it before Kristin, and I'll say it again— this whole thing stinks. Something and somebody is taking a huge risk, and I'm more and more convinced that they're trying to dump it squarely on me at the expense of my life and everyone around me.

"That's why we're going back to Canada. Someone is lying to me, and I don't like being lied to. Like I've said before, I've got to get to the bottom of this. And I know you'll be surprised to know that Bruce is helping me."

Chapter Eighteen

After their first night of sleeping on four wheels, they continued north on I-81 until they reached the Thousand Island international crossing near Alexandria Bay on the Saint Lawrence River.

"Time to put your hat and sunglasses on and lower the sun visor," John announced.

Only two vehicles were ahead of them as they approached border control. There were two uniformed Canadian agents, one inside the booth and one standing outside. John lowered his window as he slowly drove up to the booth.

"Good morning, sir. Citizenship?"

"U.S."

"And the lady?"

"Also U.S.," he answered, lifting his sunglasses to look directly at the agent, a psychological signal that he had nothing to hide.

"Passports please."

John handed him two falsified passports and waited for the agent to scan them inside the booth. He knew both would clear without any issues. He had prepared the one with Kristin's picture while they were at his cabin just for such an occasion.

The agent returned, handing the passports back to John. "Reason for your visit?"

"Just a short vacation. My lady friend has never been to Ottawa before, so I'm taking her to see your beautiful capital city."

"And how long do you expect to be in Canada?"

"Just a few days. We might go over to Montreal as well."

As the agent inside the booth presented his questions to John, the second slowly walked the length of the motor home, peeking inside the Jeep and under the RV.

"Any weapons?" The agent in the booth now seemed to be on autopilot with his questions.

"No, sir."

"Would you submit your camper to an interior walk-through inspection?"

"Certainly."

"Okay, that won't be necessary today. Have a pleasant visit. Good day."

"Thank you," John replied and lightly pressed the accelerator to ease the motor home into Canada. He looked over at Kristin, who had a nervous grin plastered on her face.

"You okay?"

"I'm shaking like a leaf."

"Why, we're just two Americans taking a little vacation with our friendly neighbor to the north. That was just a routine crossing. I knew our passports would clear, and if they wanted to search the coach, there's absolutely nothing in it that would create a problem."

"But where's your gun?"

"In the rental car back at the self-storage unit. I would never try to cross the border with it. The Canadians don't like handguns and aren't very tolerant of anyone trying to sneak one across their border."

Immediately after entering the QEW 401, John pulled off the highway into a rest area, where he made a call to Ottawa. When they were both back from using the restrooms, John told Kristin that they would be taking a short break and waiting for a return call. It came less than fifteen minutes later.

"Okay!" was all John said before he hung up and put the phone back in his pocket.

"What was that all about?"

"While you were inside, I called Emily and told her that it was extremely important that I meet with her and the prime minister as soon as possible. She went to his office to arrange a time and place. She called me back with that information."

"Well?"

"There's a provincial park along highway 416 south of Ottawa. We'll park the motor home there and take the Jeep into the city. We are to meet with them at four this afternoon in the library."

At three forty-five that afternoon, John parked the Jeep in a space he found on the street about a block from the capital. He and Kristin walked across the expansive paved area in front of the building and approached a uniformed guard with an automatic rifle strapped over her shoulder.

"We have an appointment with Minister Emily Brown," he told the young woman.

"Yes, sir, we've been expecting you. I've been instructed to escort you to the library. Follow me please."

She led them through the dark hallway that surrounded the two Chambers of Parliament where the Canadian government did its business. They entered the library and were taken to the same small room where John and Emily had first talked only a few days earlier.

"Please make yourselves comfortable," the guard said. "I will inform the minister that you have arrived. I'm sure she will be here shortly."

Kristin gazed around the beautiful library, admiring all the books and official documents lining the walls. The woodwork lining the sides and ceiling of the octagonal room was breathtaking.

"This is a beautiful place," she remarked.

"Yes, it is. It has quite a history. There's a brochure out on the reception desk. You should pick one up and read about it. There was a major fire several years ago that damn near destroyed the whole building. Quite interesting."

Just then, Emily Brown walked into the room accompanied by a man who appeared to be in his early fifties, about six feet plus a couple of inches, with a no-nonsense expression on his face. She gave John a welcoming hug and extended her hand to Kristin.

"I'm Emily Brown," she said warmly.

"Emily, this is Kristin Blake. She—"

As he was about to explain who Kristin was, the door opened and the prime minister burst into the room. He extended his hand to John, shaking it firmly and warmly.

"Prime Minister," John began. "I was about to introduce Emily to Ms. Kristin Blake. Kristin, this is Prime Minister Peter DuBois and my dear friend Emily Brown."

Before she could say a word, the prime minister lightly kissed the back of her hand. "Welcome to Ottawa Ms. Blake. I hope you have a pleasant stay in our country."

Emily took the lead, turning toward the man who entered the room with her. "John, this is Paul Featherstone. Paul is our Minister of Defense. He is responsible for all matters of security, including those concerning the prime minister. We felt that he should be included in our conversation."

"Okay. Let me explain Kristin's role in all of this. She is— or *was*— my control agent. She is the person from whom I got my instructions and to whom I reported after completing an assignment. She has been involved in the current situation from the very beginning. She has the same concerns that I have."

"Good to know," the prime minister said. "So, John, tell me what has happened since we last talked."

John explained that he had returned to Washington. He explained who Bruce was, that he had cornered him in his apartment and pressed him at gunpoint for information. He repeated, word for word, everything Bruce told him concerning the assignment, including who had ordered it. He told everyone in the room exactly all the questions he asked Bruce and the story he got in reply. For almost an hour, John detailed everything he could recall while everyone in the room sat silently listening to the twisted tale. He did not mention the part of the conversation concerning his personnel file.

"You see, Mr. Prime Minister, it was like an instant replay of the story I got from you, but with the roles of all the characters reversed. Bruce was told that you are the culprit; you are the one who is mentally unstable; and you are the one who did the dirty deed. And that's the justification for the president's order and the reason behind his actions concerning the flow of goods."

They all sat without saying a word, waiting for some sort of response from the prime minister. Finally, he spoke. "Do you think he was telling you the truth?"

"I believe he was truthfully telling me what he believes to be the truth," John answered. "As in any other situation, you don't know what you don't know. He only knows what he was told. Only you and Roger Adams know what the truth really is."

"Then the question comes down to whose story do you accept as the truth. Mine or Roger's?"

"That's exactly where we are, Mr. Prime Minister. Here's what's been rolling around in my head since I talked with Bruce. How likely is it that I get almost exactly the same story, from two different perspectives, from two supposedly honorable people? And having been told the same story from these two honorable people, how do I determine which one is truthful and which one is the liar."

"How do you know Bruce was telling you what he believed to be the truth?"

"Because he knows exactly what I do for a living, and I had a nine millimeter pistol pointed at his head the whole time we were together."

"Meaning that you believe my version of the story?"

"Sir, if I didn't believe you, I wouldn't be sitting here in this room with you. I'd be somewhere in New York City putting my plan together to assassinate you." John's statement brought a startling clarity to everyone in the room, particularly to Paul Featherstone.

"I came here to talk with you and look you in the eye to confirm what I believe to be the truth. I also wanted Kristin to see for herself, to meet and hear you, to look you in the eye and see if she believed you as well.

"Her life is now on the line, as well as mine and yours. And I happen to trust this lady as much or more than I trust anyone else," he said, pointing to Emily. "If she believes in you, that goes a very long way for me."

The prime minister looked soberly at Kristin. "Ms. Blake, what do you make of all this?"

Kristin hesitated for a moment, contemplating how she would answer. "Sir, I've been John's control officer for a number of years. Ours is a dirty business. I have had to send him all over the world to carry out assignments that will never see the light of day. He knows that before I send him on a mission, I must know that he will return safely, and that he will carry out his orders without exposing himself or our country.

"He accepts his missions knowing that I've done my job before ever assigning it to him, and that I have done everything I can to assure his safe return. Part of that job is to verify the facts, *all* the facts, concerning the assignment. I was denied the opportunity to do that with this mission. I'm sure that Mr. Featherstone will confirm that as a control officer, this is highly unusual.

"The first I knew what this assignment was, was when I took John to the first meeting with Bruce. I was stunned when I heard what they wanted him to do. We all knew that it was blatantly illegal and that there was no existing authority for such a mission. And now that I also know that Andrew is dead, I'm even more concerned with the way this has unfolded. Quite frankly, it scares the crap out of me."

She paused. "I know more about John than he knows about himself. As I said, we're in a dirty business. But to the fullest extent that honor exists in this business, I trust John to be the most honorable man I've ever known. I would, and have, placed my life in his hands."

The prime minister's eyes were locked on Kristin's face as he absorbed every word she had just spoken. He said, "And you are in love with him? You are the special woman in his life that he told Emily about?"

Kristin hesitated, her eyes filling with moisture. "Yes, sir. I've gotten to know him as a human being, as well as a government agent. What I see and what I've learned about the human side of him— Yes, sir, I have fallen in love with him."

"Objectively, do you believe you can be of sound judgment in spite of your feeling for him?"

"Absolutely, sir."

"All right!" Emily shouted. "It's about time some good woman hooked him."

John stared at Kristin in disbelief, in shock... and in total acceptance. He couldn't speak. His emotions were too strong and his self-control too lacking. He could not remember ever hearing anyone say that they loved him. He was overcome with the rush of emotion flooding his mind, his heart, and his body.

Gently, Peter DuBois placed his hand on John's arm. "Okay, where do we go from here?"

Recovering somewhat from Kristin's spontaneous announcement, John said, "Well, sir, I think you and I are going to New York City."

Paul Featherstone jumped into the conversation. "I'm sorry sir, but I can't allow that. I can't allow you to expose yourself to the possibility of becoming a target for an assassin. I don't know this man. But he clearly confessed right here that he is a professional assassin. I can't allow you to be associated with him and put yourself at risk."

"Mr. Featherstone," John interrupted. "The assassin you're justifiably worried about is sitting right here with you. I'm not going to harm the Prime Minister. I'm going to protect him. I'm going to New York to end this entire ordeal. To remove the risk he is currently exposed to."

"What will you be doing while you are there?" Featherstone asked sternly.

"Two things. First, along with your participation and that of your men, I'll be protecting the prime minister. I will not allow my country to illegally and unjustifiably take the life of our closest ally.

"Second, I can assure you that my life is in just as much jeopardy as that of your boss. I will not go through the rest of my life looking over my shoulder. I've got to root out those assigned to eliminate me and return the favor."

"And what about Roger Adams?" the prime minister asked.

Chapter Eighteen

"Don't know yet. I've got to think that through for a bit and come up with an appropriate solution. He's a primary part of my second concern. He's the leading actor in the threat to me and Kristin. You can be assured that, one way or another, I will address that issue soon."

The five people in the small room within the beautiful wood-lined library overlooking the Ottawa River and the City of Hull talked until they were satisfied that there was nothing more to talk about. They all agreed on what role each would play in the upcoming days. John explained what he would need from the Canadians. It was nearly six o'clock by the time they came to the end of their discussions.

It was agreed that the prime minister would proceed with the planned visit to New York City. Paul Featherstone would very quietly double his security force, sending undercover agents ahead to satisfy himself that he could protect his country's leader. Emily Brown would stay out front of the Canadian delegation as the primary spokesperson to minimize the prime minister's exposure, thus making Paul Featherstone's job easier. She would also be the go-between for John and the Canadian authorities.

John and Kristin would return to his undisclosed base of operation to finalize his plans and decide what to do about Bruce and Kristin's presence in the entire episode. John announced that it was time for them to leave and get some rest for the task ahead.

"You will be the guest of the Canadian government tonight. I asked Emily to arrange for a room and dinner reservations at the Chateau Laurier. I'm sure you will enjoy your stay. I would love to join you for dinner, but I think that would be unwise and draw far too much attention to you and who you are. So, I have left it in Emily's good hands. I know where I can find you if I have any further questions before you depart. If not, I will look forward to not seeing you again soon, in this life and hopefully, not in the next."

"Thank you, sir, thank you for your hospitality and most of all, for your understanding and trust."

He and Kristin walked out of the capitol building like any other tourists. They immediately blended into a group taking a tour. Reaching the sidewalk, John guided Kristin toward the left.

"Where are we going? Our car is off in the other direction."

"You heard the man! We have reservations at the Chateau."

"What's that, and where is it?"

"Right there!" he pointed. They walked across the Rideau Canal that split the city and there stood the chateau.

"Oh my gosh! It's the castle from Disney World!"

John chuckled. "Wait until you taste the food."

Chapter Nineteen

Their room registration was taken care of by Emily Brown, eliminating the need for John to produce either identification or a credit card for payment. They were led by a bellman to their room overlooking the river and the canal.

There was a nervous, flittering few minutes for John once they found themselves alone in their room. There was a brand new elephant in the room being led around by Kristin's proclamation of her feelings. She sat on the edge of the bed while he made himself busy doing nothing.

"John, come sit by me."

"Well, I have to—"

"John!" she insisted.

He finally sat next to her without making any contact with her body and without looking her in the eye. He was back to being a little boy facing up to the first girl he ever kissed.

"Let's talk," Kristin said.

"Okay," he said, his fingers twisting the edge of the quilt innocently draped over the bed.

"John," Kristin began, tilting her face in front of his so he would have to look at her. "I know what I said surprised you, but I meant every word. I have found, much to my surprise, that I have fallen completely and utterly in love with you. But, I understand our situation and don't expect you to change anything about our—"

He abruptly turned, taking her face in his two hands and kissing her firmly. She was caught by surprise, startled by his move until she felt the warmth and tenderness of his lips. Losing control, she melted to his touch, returning the kiss with passion.

"Kristin," he said, as he pulled back slightly from the kiss. Looking into her eyes while still cradling her face he said, "That is the first time in my adult life that I have ever heard anyone say those words...either to me or about me.

"I was...I am so frightened of you. So frightened of the way I feel for you. I don't know how to express myself. All I know is that my head, my heart, my stomach—everything inside me right now feels like my body is a blender on high speed."

He paused again, still holding her face close to his. "I know I have never felt this way toward anyone. I've never had anyone make me feel this way. When you said you loved me, I— I couldn't breathe.

Chapter Nineteen

"This time that we've spent together has been a new experience for me. All I want to do is be with you. When we were driving to Ottawa, I didn't want to get here. All I wanted to do was to keep driving with you next to me.

"I've never been allowed to be in love. I've never been allowed to get close enough or even to be with a person long enough to fall in love. Or even to know what love is. So, if what I'm going through right now is love then— then I guess I'm in love with you too!"

She threw her arms around his neck and pulled him to her, embracing him with all her strength. They fell onto the bed smothering each other with kisses. Pulling at each other's clothing until finally they were skin to skin.

Their lovemaking didn't last long. It couldn't. They were both overcome with such strong desire that reaching an orgasm was not the climax of their act. It was more like taking another breath during a full day of breathing. Being together, acknowledging their love for one another, being in contact with each other: that was what was important and satisfying and fulfilling, completing the physical act with such tenderness that it simply became the glue binding them together.

They never got to go out for dinner. Instead, they ordered room service and ate sitting together dressed only in two fluffy white terry robes provided by the hotel. They laughed and giggled and touched and kissed, isolated in their new world, finally falling asleep in each other's arms.

After breakfast, they left the chateau and walked back to their Jeep. On the way, John placed a call to Emily to thank her for the wonderful accommodations she had arranged for them.

During the conversation, he also asked her to provide a Canadian diplomatic pass to get him into the events that would be held in New York City during the upcoming meetings. He would contact her in New York to arrange getting it from her. Then, returning to the motor home, John re-attached the Jeep to the RV and began the drive back to the U.S.

"Where are we going?" Kristin asked him.

"We're going back to the cabin, but we'll take a different route. Two people on vacation would likely use different crossing points. We need to tour this great country a little more to make it appear that we really are on vacation. We'll head toward Montreal and then south. We'll re-enter the U.S. in Vermont. It's a bit longer, but I would feel better if we did it that way."

They traveled along QEW 401 to the Ontario-Quebec border, where it changed to Route 20. He followed 20, crossing the Saint Lawrence on the Pont Champlain bridge, then picked his way south to Route 133 until it approached the U.S. border at the north end of I-89 in Vermont.

They crossed the border with the same degree of ease they experienced entering Canada the day before. Far more attention was being paid to a moose hit and killed by a trailer truck than to an international assassin crossing from one country to another.

"That sure was easy," Kristin commented. "I can see why we have such a problem with immigration and security."

"Yeah. At least now you have to have a passport. A few years ago, all you needed was a smile."

Chapter Nineteen

They continued south on I-89 to Burlington, where John changed over to route 7, picking his way south through the Vermont farmlands along the less-traveled highway. They crossed the lower tail of Lake Champlain at Crown Point, driving back into New York State.

A short time later, Kristin saw a road sign with an arrow pointing to Ticonderoga.

"Wait, isn't that—?"

"Yeah, yeah, that's the one I can't spell."

"Didn't I see a sign saying that there was a fort at Crown Point?"

"Yes, you did, and I can spell Crown Point just fine."

"What's the difference between the two...besides the spelling?" she teased.

"Both date back to the era of colonization. Ticonderoga was the more successful of the two and changed hands between the two sides, the English and the patriots. Crown Point doesn't have the same history because of where it was built. It was too easy to outflank.

"Ticonderoga has been restored and is now a big tourist attraction. Crown Point has been preserved, but nothing has been done with it, like adding attractions or reenactments. It's just there."

"Which do you like better?"

"They're totally different. You can go to Ticonderoga and get a lesson in American history by touring the grounds and taking in all the activities offered there. To appreciate Crown Point, you need to know the history before you go. It's stark and eerie. I love it, especially right at dawn or dusk. You can feel the ghosts walking beside you and feel them living amongst the buildings and see them guarding the ramparts surrounding the parade field."

"Will you take me to see both?"

"Kristin, when this crap we're dealing with is over, I'll take you wherever you want to go!"

She leaned back in her seat with a satisfied grin tattooed across her face. She was happier than she had ever been. She rode along, savoring the views of the Adirondacks to the west and the rolling hills of the Champlain Valley to the east. The only thing disturbing her was the knowledge that it would soon be over...at least for a while.

John drove south, picking his way across the hills and valleys until he finally reached I-87, better known in this area as the Northway. Once on it, he drove south, exiting in Queensbury, adjacent to Glens Falls. At the intersection of Route 9, he turned north until he reached Great Escape, an amusement park, not far from the outlets they had shopped at a few days earlier.

He turned into the park and pulled his rig into the area provided for RV's, positioning the motor home between two units already parked. He got out and unhooked the Jeep from rig. He knew his unit would disappear among the sea of motor homes, travel trailers, and fifth wheelers awaiting the return of the families now enjoying the gut-twisting high-speed rides.

He also knew that the Pennsylvania license plates on the coach would not attract any attention. His plates would blend into all the others from all over the northeast and beyond.

After getting the Jeep road-ready, he sent a one-word text message to Bob, letting him know that he was about to return to the compound and needed to have the gate opened. Thirty minutes later, they glided past the steel barrier where Bob stood, waiting for them to clear before he locked the cement-filled six-inch steel pipe behind them. John waited for Bob to approach his vehicle.

"Welcome home."

"Thanks Bob. Everything okay?"

"Yep, all's well. Bruce and I connected okay. He was a bit nervous during the whole process. Once I got him and his family all settled in, the mountains and the lake worked their magic on him. He's relaxed now and doing fine. Oh, and he can't spell worth a crap either."

"Where is he?"

"I have them staying in your cabin in the loft bedrooms. I think right now they're down by the lake sucking in the sunset."

"Okay, we'll get settled in the cabin. It's been a long day. Could you please ask him to join us? I'd also like you there. We need to talk."

Twenty minutes later, following an awkward reunion between Kristin and Bruce, the group was gathered in the den of the cabin. Bruce's family was asked to wait at Bob's while they met.

"Make yourselves comfortable," John said. "I think we're going to be here for a while. I'll start."

John, knowing that he was the only one of the four who had been a party to all the meetings and conversations of the past few days, began by reviewing the entire period from the first telephone call from Kristin right up to the present moment. He knew parts would be repetitive to some, but he needed to repeat the entire story to be sure that everyone had all the information.

He took his time, being sure to provide as much detail as possible, while keeping to himself his personal reaction to the events that had taken place. He didn't want to influence the thoughts of the others. He wanted them to give the group their individual, untainted reaction.

After completing his portrayal of the events, he leaned back in his chair, signaling that the floor was now open for the others to speak.

"Questions?"

Bruce spoke first. "Why do you want me here, and what do you expect me to do?"

"Well, I think that each of us has a contribution to make," John began. "First, Bob is the only one of us who has had no real active role in the entire situation. However, Bob and I go a long way back. We served together in the military, and he was once a candidate to become an agent in the same service I'm in. He knows the ropes and understands how these things work. If it weren't for an unfortunate injury, he might well be the person sitting in my chair. So, he knows what is needed, and I trust his opinion and advice.

"Second, Kristin, having been my control for years, knows all there is to know about how mission assignments are developed and assigned. She knows all the players inside the agency and their individual roles in the game. And she has potentially important contacts we might need.

"Third, Bruce. You're the bureaucrat. You know where the missions originate and how they flow down through the system until they get to agents. And, in this case, it seems that you might very well become a more integral part of the mission.

"Here's what I want us to brainstorm without any reservations. No questions are too minor to ask and no suggestion or idea too small to offer. Got it?"

Three heads nodded in response.

"Okay. Bruce, let me start off with you. Why? Why would this mission ever have been considered and by whom?"

"Well, like I told you when we were in my apartment, this came from the top."

"The top! Exactly what are you saying?"

"Given the route and method this took to get to me, the person who spoke to me, and the directions I was given, if I had to stake my life on it, which it seems that I might be doing, I'd say this came directly from the president."

"From the president?"

"Yes."

"Okay, next question. Why? Why would the President of the United States directly order the assassination of the Prime Minister of Canada?"

Bruce paused for a moment, digesting the question and measuring his answer. "Based on what I was told, and hearing what you had to say about the story you got from the prime minister, it's clear one of them is lying. If you feel certain that it's the president who's doing the lying, then my guess is that he's trying to cover his ass.

"The prime minister is the only person who can expose his past and potentially ruin his reputation and destroy his career. You know how these guys worry about their legacy. They're paranoid over it. They see themselves in the history books and will do anything to make themselves go down in history as..."

"...as the ultimate good guy," John finished.

"Yes. That's a good way of putting it," Bruce added.

"But why now?" Kristin asked. "Why after all these years would he take such a drastic and illegal action? It's been well over twenty years since the two of them were in college together. Peter DuBois has never divulged anything that would threaten the president."

Bob jumped in. "The prime minister hinted that the president has some emotional problems. Maybe he's gotten to the point where he can't control himself. Maybe there's more to his condition and it's manifesting itself and he's losing control."

"It was more than a hint, and it was more like mental issues than simply being emotional," John corrected. "The PM said that these issues have been covered up by his father and all the politicos that have been close to him. Seems they have been doing it for years. Dealing with it for a big part of his career."

"But if that's the case," Bob asked, "is he really the one coming up with this crazy idea, or is it someone close to him? Someone who is dependent upon him to protect him and his position? Someone close to him who is really the power behind the office?"

"You mean like someone sucking on his political teat?" John asked.

"Exactly!"

"If that were the case," Kristin jumped in, "then whoever this person is, is totally dependent on the president's position and power. If he is taken out of power, so goes the fate of those depending on him."

"Right again," Bob said.

"Bruce," John directed himself to the Washington insider. "If we're guessing correctly, my next question is how do they think they would ever get away with such a harebrained idea? How do they think the whole thing wouldn't fall right back in their lap?"

Again, Bruce paused, his head dropping down while he contemplated his answer. "Let me qualify something here.

After listening to this whole story, I don't think it's *they*. I think it's *he*."

"And by *he*, I take it you mean William Baxter, the Chief of Staff?"

"Exactly! If you look back over his career and his attachment to the president, he's the only person I see pulling the strings.

"Back to your question, I have a two-part answer, John. First is arrogance. These people think that they are so far above everyone else that they can do anything they want and answer to no one. They believe that everyone else in the country will believe whatever they say. If you're looking at a white wall and they say it's black, then it's black and all the little people will believe it and will buy it. They believe they can get away with anything.

"So, if they get caught hatching a plan like this and deny it, in their minds, that's the end of it. The world will believe them simply because of who they are. It is extraordinarily difficult to understand the level of arrogance these people bring to Washington. They firmly believe, as delusional as it might be, that once the people of the country vote them into office, they are superior to everyone. They totally believe that the rest of the citizens of the country are just a bunch of dumbass cattle waiting and willing to be led to the slaughter."

"And second?" asked John.

"Second is you!" he said, looking directly at John. "They know who you are. They picked you from a list of field agents. They have never met you, but they think they know you just by reading your file.

Chapter Nineteen

"They see you as a dinosaur. A dangerous dinosaur. You've been around too long. You have been on too many missions and have too much knowledge. You know where all the secrets are buried. Therefore, you are dangerous. So, how best to eliminate you? To kill two birds with one stone, so to speak.

"I'm certain that the plan is—or was—to have you go on a hairy-assed mission like this and then expose you. Their order to me was to have you make the prime minister's death appear to be from natural causes. But that was a hoax.

"Little by little, they planned on leaking tiny bits of information, dispelling the natural causes crap. Ultimately it would all lead to you. The professional assassin who made the PM's death look like it was natural. They would hold you up to the world, saying, 'Look, we found the killer of the prime minister. We got him. We're the good guys. You become the evil villain. Certainly not the president.'

"Then what? Did they expect me to keep my mouth shut? To take one for the Gipper?"

"You would never have the chance to say anything, John. Like I said, you were being set up. When I say they planned on holding you up as the bad guy, what I should say is they intended to hold up your limp, dead body. Put you on display. Tacked to a board leaning up against the Okay Corral like in the old westerns.

"There are at least two other agents who would be assigned to take you out. That would be the final act. You would be the final act. Your dead body being displayed on CNN and MSNBC and Fox. That would be the final curtain, and they would make their next move."

The room was dead silent following Bruce's comments. Kristin choked back her fright and her tears. She looked across the room at John. He stared at the floor. It was Bob who broke the silence.

"Fear! Fear of being exposed. Fear and paranoia. He knows that DuBois holds the secret to his downfall. He fears that the PM might someday, sometime, somehow use it against him. Ruin his life and his career. DuBois has power over him, and he can't deal with that. He can't accept that and just leave it out there. He must do something about it. That's why all of this is taking place.

"The whole Saint Lawrence Seaway thing is his way of justifying all of this in his own mind. A way for him to justify that he is doing this to protect the United States. A way for him to believe that he is doing this because it's his job as president to protect this country."

"You mean kill the source," Kristin said.

"I mean kill the source. Kill the threat. And exploit the outcome."

"Wow!" Kristin said. "That's wild."

John stepped in. "This whole bullshit story about the flow of trade on the Saint Lawrence is his way of justifying to himself what he is up to. It's a hoax. It isn't a strong enough case to justify a murder."

"But Baxter won't buck him?" Bob said.

"No," Bruce interjected. "He won't buck him because Roger is the golden goose. He's Baxter's ticket on the express train they all ride. He's the ticket to political nirvana."

Chapter Nineteen

Bob came to his friend's side. "John, this whole thing is so far-fetched it makes absolutely no sense at all. The whole thing about trade on the Saint Lawrence is so trumped up I can't believe they think anyone will buy this. It's Canada, for Christ sake.

"You've got to get yourself out of this somehow. You have no idea who's after you, where they will try to take you out. Nothing! You go through with this, you're a dead man."

John didn't say a word. He sat on the couch with his hands clasped together, his chin resting on his knuckles. Finally, he spoke. He looked at Bruce.

"Did you get me the information I asked you for?"

"Yes."

"And the other thing we talked about?"

"Done!"

"Well then, how do you feel about going back to D.C.?"

"Not good. What do you have in mind?"

"I'm not totally sure yet. And, beyond this meeting, I don't think it's wise that I share my thoughts with the three of you. I've got to come up with a plan, and it cannot include any of you. Getting anywhere near this would expose each of you and make you a potential target. I can't allow that. From here on out, this is my mission.

"What I would ask you to consider, Bruce, is going back to D.C. and acting as if nothing had happened. That we have never met, and you know nothing about my meetings in Canada. We'll get you back there through Pittsburgh so it looks like you were visiting with your dad.

"Leave your family here where we can look after them. Then all I'd ask you to do is let it be known that I reported in and that I'm in New York preparing to carry out the assignment."

"And then what?" Bruce asked.

"Take a long vacation. Come back up here as quickly and as quietly as you can. We'll keep your family here under wraps. Bob and I will set up a place for you to live long term. He'll get you in here without the rest of the world knowing where you are or what you're doing."

"I have another idea," Bob broke in. "To avoid potential trouble and distraction, why not have Bruce call in and tell his office that his father's illness was a false alarm. But while he's out there, he wants to extend his stay for a week or so."

"I like that better," Bruce said. "I'm afraid that if I go back to D.C., I will be too nervous to convince anyone that all was well. I'm afraid I couldn't pull it off, and that would send a bad signal."

"Okay, we'll do it that way. Except you're going to have to place that call from somewhere near Pittsburgh. If our mysterious friends decide to trace where your call came from, it must have generated from a tower in Pennsylvania. Not Upstate New York. Not anywhere near here. It can't lead them back here."

"We can arrange for that," Bob said. "If need be, I can drive Bruce to Erie to make the call. We can be there and back in less than a day. We can use the extra time to get housing set up for Bruce and his family. The Jacobs house is available. They notified me that they wouldn't be back here at all this year."

"Done!" John said.

This time it was Kristin who spoke up. "And then what, John? You can't possibly intend to complete the assignment? What will you do in New York?"

"Like I said, I'm not completely sure yet. And when I am, I can't share that with any of you. From here on out, I have to deal with this alone."

"Are you fucking crazy?" Kristin blurted out. "Excuse my French, but you're walking into a trap. You need all the help you can get."

"Kristin!" John reacted, trying not to chuckle at her language outburst.

"I agree with her," Bob added.

"Bob, you know what your job is. This compound is where you need to be. I need a safe place to come back to. You've provided that for me for years. This isn't the first time I've gone into something with the odds stacked against me.

"And besides, I need you to take care of Kristin and the rest of our new family. When I get back, I want to see these beautiful faces. Including the one with the new-found potty mouth. I need to know she's in good hands so I don't have to worry about her while I'm taking care of business."

"But—!" Kristin said, flushing a bright pink.

"No buts, damn it!" John said sternly. "That's the way it is. That's the way it must be. You are not a field agent, and I don't have the time to make you into one. What I need from you is to stay here and to stay safe.

"You, of all people, know damned well, as the man once said, 'This is not my first rodeo.' I've been down this road before and I can't be distracted by my feelings for you once I'm in the middle of a mission. I've got to know you are safe. I'll get it done, and I'll get back here in one piece. That's all I need you to believe."

Chapter Twenty

At four thirty the next morning, Bob and Bruce left for the drive to Erie, Pennsylvania to make the planned telephone call that would set the stage for John's plan.

After a tense breakfast during which John and Kristin exchanged nothing more than a few grunts, he slipped into his room and proceeded to pack a bag with the clothes and equipment needed for him to complete his task.

In the bedroom, he moved the bed about three feet to the side, exposing the floor underneath. He lifted a nearly invisible trapdoor hidden under the bed. Concealed under the floor was a sealed, watertight compartment containing his tactical equipment, including firearms, multiple sets of identification, miscellaneous equipment, and substantial amounts of cash in several international currencies.

He took what he needed and placed it in a small duffel bag. Returning to the kitchen, he found Kristin still sitting at the table fidgeting with her now-empty coffee cup. He took her by the hand and led her to the nearby couch.

He took her hands in his and held them firmly, knowing that this might be the last time he ever saw her.

"Kristin," he began. "I've never said this to any other woman in my entire life. I love you. More deeply and strongly than I ever imagined possible."

She tried to speak, but he placed his hand over her mouth to silence her.

"Please let me finish or I might never be able to get this out. "You have to be confident in me. Confident that what I'm telling you is true and…confident that you give me an entirely new reason for coming back here to you.

"What I do, what I have done for this country would leave most people feeling disgusted. But I love this country and in my mind, I am a patriot. I do what I do because I believe it's necessary. It's my way of protecting what I believe in. I hope you can understand that and accept that. And I hope that it never comes between us in any way.

"I will promise you one thing... no, two things. First, this will be my last mission. I'm done. I've done enough. I have too many of these missions under my belt. I'm getting to the point where my sharpness is just not the same. So I need to quit. I don't want to do this anymore. For the first time, I feel as if it is destroying me. It won't be easy. This is not a job with a retirement plan built into the benefit package.

"Second, I promise you I will come back, and I'll do my best to come back in one piece. All I want to know is that you'll be here when I come back. If you can't, I'll understand. If you are here, well…I have some promises to keep, including a long weekend at the Sagamore."

Chapter Twenty

Tears filled her eyes. Not tears of sorrow. Tears of joy, tears of love. Tears of happiness and anticipation of what the future held. She couldn't talk. Her emotions blocked her every attempt to speak. She tried to choke back her feelings long enough to respond to John, but she could only squeeze out two words.

"Come back!"

John took the rest of the day to drive back to his motor home parked at the amusement park, re-attach his Jeep, and drive to Philadelphia, where he returned the coach and Jeep to the storage facility and picked up the rental car that he and Kristin had left behind a few days earlier. Then he drove to the Philadelphia airport, where he turned the car in at the appropriate rental agency.

He returned to the city center of Philadelphia and took a train to Penn Station. Donning a baseball cap and sunglasses, he ducked all the security cameras as he made his way through the station to 34th street, where he hailed a cab to take him crosstown to Grand Central. He stashed his duffel bag in a locker, exited the station, and walked east toward the United Nations building on the East River. For the next three hours, he walked back and forth from north to south and back again, repeatedly passing by the building, studying every possible approach. His surveillance convinced him that this was not where he would carry out the plan formulating in his mind.

Satisfied, he returned to Grand Central on 42nd Street and caught the next train north to Tarrytown, where he found a motel with an available room, ate dinner at a nearby pizza restaurant, and settled in for the night. He very much wanted to call Kristin and hear her voice, but he knew he would be putting them both at risk by doing so.

The Salesman

All the international delegations would begin to arrive the following day. The major sessions of the General Assembly wouldn't take place for two more days. This schedule gave him sufficient time to finalize the plans coming together in his mind.

After a restless night, during which the pieces of his plan all fell into place, he paid cash for another two nights in the motel and caught a train back to Midtown, where he again walked to the U.N building, repeating his survey of the previous day to confirm his observations.

Once he had, he walked back to Grand Central, entering from 42nd Street, crossing the main lobby, and taking the escalators to the upper level, where he left the building. He entered the pedestrian tunnel on the west side of the Helmsley Building, emerging on Park Avenue.

He walked north a couple of blocks until he was directly across from the Waldorf Astoria. This was where the reception for the dignitaries, including Prime Minister Peter DuBois of Canada and President Roger Adams of the United States, would be held.

He knew that by midday, security at the hotel would be tighter than a gnat's ass, so he needed to enter the hotel now to survey the lobby area. Once again wearing a ball cap and sunglasses, he walked back toward the Helmsley Building, crossed over the divided traffic lanes of Park Avenue and continued along 47th street until he reached Lexington Avenue. There he turned back to the north to approach the second, less used, entrance to the famed hotel.

He passed through the doorway and ascended the stairs up to the main level. He took a seat in one of the cushioned armchairs near the lobby lounge area and studied the interior of the hotel. He could easily identify the plain-clothes security agents already inside the hotel. He could determine which country some represented simply by looking at their clothing or shoes. They were doing pretty much the same thing he was doing, except for an entirely different purpose.

They were studying faces to identify anyone known or suspected to be a security risk. He was there to memorize the floor plan and escape routes. After an hour, having moved to different chairs several times so as not to draw the attention of any of the agents on duty, he slowly made his way toward the main ballroom where the reception would be held.

It was an enormous room. In a couple of days, it would be packed with people from around the world, including hundreds of members of the international press and hundreds more security personnel. He couldn't linger near the entrance for fear of drawing attention to himself.

Finally, he felt that he had the information he needed and returned to the lobby. There he turned toward the west, leaving the hotel through the revolving doors leading out to Park Avenue. Back on the sidewalk, he turned south and walked to the train terminal.

He knew that Grand Central, the largest train station in the world, would offer him ample opportunity to lose himself in the crowds and the maze of passageways. There were exits on all four sides of the terminal at various levels. Plus, there were stairways leading to the train platforms and subway tracks that ran underneath the building and the streets of Manhattan.

The Salesman

It was approaching late afternoon. His last act of the day was to indulge himself by buying a world-famous Nathan's Hot Dog loaded with yellow mustard and sauerkraut. He felt that he owed himself a moment to be human.

He took a seat on one of the benches in the middle of the lobby to enjoy the odor and flavor of his treat while taking in the flow of pedestrian traffic. He sat eating his hot dog, acting like a longtime New Yorker, not giving a rat's ass for anyone else in the world.

Satisfied, he boarded a northbound train to Westchester County and his motel room in Tarrytown. Following a few enjoyable and smelly burps resulting from his sauerkraut-loaded treat, he sat quietly reviewing everything he had taken in during the past couple of days.

Now it was time to finalize his plan. He had work to do and only a little over one day to get it all completed. And he had to go shopping.

Chapter Twenty-One

The next morning the early news was flooded with video of the foreign delegations arriving in Manhattan: Great Britain, France, Germany, Brazil, Italy, Russia, Australia, Japan, and Canada—over a hundred leaders representing most of the developed world, plus the third world contingent, who came to hear how the powerful would rule the roost.

John watched Fox, switching to NBC, then CBS and ABC, listening to each network's bias toward the conferences to be held over the next few days.

While out shopping the previous evening, he had walked into the lobby of a motel a couple of blocks from the one he was staying in. Using a public telephone, he dialed Emily Brown's private cell number. She answered on the second ring.

"Hello," she said.

"Em, it's Charles."

"Charles, it's so good to hear from you. Where are you?"

"I'm in town. Here for the big to-do at the U.N." John answered in a very plausible British accent. "How's mum?"

"She's doing just fine. Will I get to see you while you're here, little brother?"

"I hope so, Em. Are you staying at the embassy with the prime minister?"

"Yes. Most of the delegation is there. How about you? Where are you staying?"

"We haven't checked into a hotel yet. Hope to find something close by. We'd love to see you. I'll be in Midtown tomorrow about three. Would it be all right if I stopped by the embassy for a moment to say hello?"

"That would be great, Charles. I'll meet you at the main entrance to get you through security. How does that sound?"

"Wonderful, Em. I'll see you then. Cheers!"

"Bye-bye, Charles. See you tomorrow."

Meeting set. She would meet him at the entrance to the Canadian embassy at nine o'clock in the morning, not at three in the afternoon. It would be three hours before noon instead of three hours after noon. Then she would return to the entrance at three, looking as if she were waiting for someone who failed to show up, just in case anyone was watching.

Chapter Twenty-One

When he approached the embassy entrance in the morning, she would give him the Canadian diplomatic invitation to the ceremonies to be held the day after at the Waldorf. He would temporarily assume a Canadian identity and citizenship. He had all the necessary supporting documents in his little duffel bag.

Today would be spent in his room preparing himself for what was to come early the following evening in the heart of the Big Apple. He took all the items he had purchased on his shopping spree the day before and began putting together everything he felt he would need to be successful.

His training, experience, and discipline all began to kick in. There was no room in his mind for anything else, including Kristin. He had to force her from his mind until he completed what he was about to do. Thinking of her would be a distraction, and in his business distractions got you killed.

He had retrieved his duffel bag from the locker in Grand Central; along with all the items he had bought locally, he began putting the pieces together. One thing for sure, he knew he could not carry a gun with him. He would never get past the security at the entrance to the hotel. But guns were far from being the only weapon he had at his disposal. He had taken a variety of items from the chamber beneath his bed. He had settled on his final method.

By dinnertime he had almost completed his preparations. He found a take-out menu in the desk drawer in his room and ordered Chinese. When it arrived, he sat cross-legged on his bed and watched more of the network news programs to see if anything unusual had taken place during the day concerning all the diplomatic arrivals.

The Salesman

Everything being reported was as expected. The New York City police department delivered its usual excellent level of performance. Crowd and traffic control were handled with no confusion or incidents. The men and women in blue knew exactly what to do and how to deal with this onslaught of outsiders.

Following his usual habit, John took a non-narcotic over-the-counter sleep aid to help him get some rest. He did this because he knew that if he didn't, he would be too anxious to sleep and he needed his rest to be sharp and alert the next day. He couldn't afford to get sloppy due to the lack of a few hours of sleep.

By nine o'clock, his eyes began to droop and his head nodded from side to side. At nine fifteen, he gave up the fight, turning off the TV and bedside lamp, and sliding down to rest his head on the pillow.

By seven thirty the next morning he was standing on the station platform waiting for the next southbound train to take him back into Manhattan. He had his duffel bag over one shoulder and carried a second smaller bag, more like a purse, in his left hand.

When he arrived at Grand Central, he again stashed the larger bag in a locker and took only the smaller bag with him. From the terminal, he made his way to 42nd street and turned left. Not far from the entrance was a large office building housing the headquarters of an international pharmaceutical company.

In the center of the lobby was a circular reception desk with two uniformed security guards staring at monitors. Next to the guard on the right was an open box containing visitor passes. He waited until someone approached the guard for information. After a short conversation, the woman was handed a pass.

As she stepped away from the desk, John purposefully stepped in her path, bumping her head on.

"Excuse me, miss. I'm sorry, I wasn't looking where I was walking."

The woman never said a word and barely looked at John... nor did she take notice that her visitor's badge was no longer dangling from the front of her blouse.

John took a casual lap around the lobby to blend in and disappear in the crowd. In a corner near a utility closet, he turned his back to the reception desk and attached the visitors pass to his shirt pocket. As nonchalantly as he could, he walked toward the bank of elevators in the center of the lobby. He drew no notice from the security guards.

He boarded an elevator, exiting on the tenth floor, where he saw another reception desk. He approached and asked the young woman seated with her head down intently studying her cell phone if she could direct him to a restroom. She did so without breaking her concentration on her electronic device.

John found the restroom. On the door was mounted the stick figure symbol signifying that the room was usable by either male or female gender. Perfect!

John entered as an attractive six-foot-three man in his late thirties. Twenty minutes later, a rather large, hunched over gray-haired sixty-year-old woman dressed in a non-threatening dark blue two-piece outfit, leaning on a cane, and wearing eyeglasses emerged from the gender-neutral restroom. She carried a small duffel bag looped over her shoulder. Even his mother, wherever she might be, wouldn't have recognized him.

He retraced his steps back to the elevator, not drawing one iota of attention from the young woman mesmerized by the earth-shaking information pouring from her cell phone. She had to be immersed in some sort of deep intellectual revelation demanding one hundred percent of her brain power to ignore her duties of guarding the lobby area. John smiled his thanks toward her oblivion and invisibly slipped into the elevator.

Back on the street, he stood erect, once again altering his appearance. He began walking with full stride toward the Canadian embassy. At eight fifty-five, he was standing across the street from the entrance when he saw the front door open and Emily Brown step out. He knew she would not be looking for an old scrunched-up woman so he stepped off the curb to cross the street toward her.

She was looking in both directions for the man she was to meet, ready to hand off the small envelope she held in her grasp. Instead, she noticed a rather large older woman approaching her with an uncommonly long and athletic stride. As the older woman drew near, there was something vaguely familiar about her that caught Emily's attention.

"John?"

"Walk with me."

John slipped his arm inside Emily's as if the old woman he had become needed a little support to walk. He led Emily away from the front entrance of the embassy, rounding the corner at the end of the block.

Chapter Twenty-One

"John!" she said again. "What...? Why...?"

"Good morning, Emily. Please don't ask questions I can't answer for you. Have you got the invitation I asked for?"

"Yes," she said, handing him the envelope. "This will get you into the hotel as well as into any of the events taking place there."

"Good...and thank you. Now, here's what I would like you to tell the prime minister. Once he arrives at the reception later today, he's going to come down with an upset stomach. A very bad upset stomach. He'll want to return to the embassy immediately."

"But, what about the official dinner?"

"There will be no dinner for him. Not tonight. He needs to be too sick to stay for dinner and he must return to the embassy because of his illness."

"But why, John?"

"Emily, I told you I can't answer your questions. But I will tell you this, there is a second agent, possibly even two others who are somewhere close by. Their job is to make sure that I carry out my assignment. Once they see that I have not, they will attempt to kill the prime minister. So, he can't be where they can do that. He must unexpectedly change his schedule and return to the embassy. He needs to be secure. I'm sure Mr. Featherstone will understand and agree."

"What about you? What are you going to do? Where will you be?"

The Salesman

He leaned over and kissed her on the cheek. "I'll see you in Ottawa soon." He turned and walked away, leaving her standing on the sidewalk in New York City with her questions dangling, unanswered.

Chapter Twenty-Two

After leaving Emily, John walked crosstown to Park Avenue and made his way to his favorite Oriental restaurant on 49th street, east of Park. It was too early to enter for lunch so he walked up and down the streets, observing all the security preparations being made for the event that would take place later in the day.

New York City, like Washington, D.C., was accustomed to having everyday life interrupted by some sort of an event. Those people who lived in the greater metropolitan area surrounding the city and traveled here every morning to take advantage of the lucrative jobs were not frazzled at all by today's events. Neither were the fantastic and oft maligned men and women of the NYPD. They protected this vast metropolitan area with a rare dedication to duty. All personnel seemed to take things in stride like no other city in the world.

This was Mecca for everyone looking to have their names plastered across the evening news. For those in the world of entertainment, where all the wannabes try to rub elbows with those already of star status. And for all the second-tier-athletes, no matter what type of ball they played with. This was the capital of visibility. This was where they came to stir up their own little moment in the spotlight. Their fifteen minutes of fame. This was where the little "shining-light on the hill" got turned on...or off.

New Yorkers have been accused of being able to step over a dead boy lying on the sidewalk. Maybe that was true, maybe it wasn't. But what was true was the total disdain with which they dealt with the self-inflated and self-indulgent who so often created a minor ripple in their everyday routine. Every one of them was far too self-important to be bothered by anyone else.

John's day moved slowly. Time always seems to slow down when waiting. He had little to do except watch the preparations being made to protect many who didn't need protecting: those who fit into the category of "legends in their own minds." If he was looking for anything in these activities, it was for what was not normal. Measures being taken or faces that, for some reason, looked out of place or didn't belong. Anyone too nervous and jittery. Or someone doing something unusual. Exhibiting quirky moves or displaying questionable facial expressions. Or watching him too closely.

These would be the things that would reveal those who might create a danger to him. Those who tried their hardest to blend in, very often were those who stuck out the most. He had to see if he could identify the men assigned to take out him or the prime minister of Canada, should he fail to complete his assignment.

He had no intention of assassinating Peter DuBois. He was unswervingly focused on trying to identify anyone who might be assigned to assassinating him. His focus was now on survival and for the first time in his life, his own personal future.

He knew by not carrying out this mission that his life as an agent was over. Done with. And he was okay with that. He had enough money to last the rest of his life and assure the safety of all those now within his personal circle. Money was of no concern to him at all.

But what he now had for the first time was someone who cared for him and for whom he cared equally. That was a new consideration. He also knew that by not fulfilling his mission, by just walking away from it, he would set up a whole new set of conditions. He didn't want to be living the rest of his life with Kristin constantly looking over his shoulder for someone, anyone with the intent to kill him.

There were two ways out of this predicament. One was to eliminate those assigned to kill him and the second was to eliminate the mission in its entirety. That was his reason for risking entering the Waldorf Astoria and standing on the reception line. He knew from his years of experience that once the head of a snake was cut off, the rest of the snake would wither away.

For once, he wanted to be seen. He planned on entering the hotel early enough to be seen and photographed by the security cameras that would surely be covering every square inch of the lobby. He wanted the old lady, hunched over and leaning on her cane, to be seen and recorded.

He also knew that he would have to stay long enough to be recorded on film after the main event had begun. He did not want it to appear that he was there for the arrival of just one person. His interest, his only real interest, was

Roger Adams, President of the United States. He wanted to look the man dead in the eye, the man who chose his name from a list scribbled on a piece of paper. The man who so very casually was setting him up to be killed to cover his own sick presidential ass.

When the time came, he changed his appearance slightly by bending a bit at the waist, hunching his shoulders and leaning on a cane. The security teams, along with the NYPD, had already diverted all traffic from Park Avenue north of 47th street up to 54th. What he needed most now was to look like just another New Yorker walking the streets.

He approached the front door to the hotel and presented his Canadian diplomatic credentials to the security personnel. They passed him through with no difficulty. Once inside, he found a restroom to complete his disguise. As he approached the restrooms, he suddenly remembered that he had to enter the ladies' room and not the men's since he, for the moment, was a woman.

When he had completed his preparations, he made his way to the same lounge area he had sat in a few days earlier. He observed the bustle and hustle of activity in the lobby. While in the ladies' room, he had added a couple of finishing touches to his outfit. He now had on a generic pillbox hat, rather like that worn by Jackie Kennedy. To that, he added a light gray veil that he pulled down over his face to blend with the five o'clock shadow that would surely tip off his identity.

Second, he added white gloves common to the era of a woman dressed like he was. She might very well wear gloves to a dress-up affair like this. With the combination of hat and gloves, he looked far more like a country school-marm than an assassin.

Time dragged by until it was finally time for those with the proper credentials to gather in the main ballroom. Many joined the welcoming line so they could tell their grandchildren that they had shaken the hands of the power brokers temporarily running the world.

John took his place in line and waited. Minor dignitaries from equally minor countries of equally minor importance began to flow in. He pleasantly shook the hand of each while scanning the room for telltale signs of potential danger. He couldn't pick anyone that he saw as a threat out of the crowd.

Some of those entering the ballroom where dressed in the elaborate costumes native to their country, especially the women. Their outfits were spectacular, with bright colors and towering head pieces that left him to wonder how they kept them atop their heads. Some of the men were also attired in elaborate costumes of their native lands, but paled in comparison with the women.

At last, the big guys began to arrive. First, it was the Germans, followed closely by the Russians, and then the French. They were followed by a lull in the activities until the crowd suddenly reacted. A bustle of activity erupted near the entrance. Roger Adams had arrived, with all the expected turmoil that followed his presence everywhere.

It took an exorbitant amount of time and effort for things to return to a normal level of confusion. Security personnel scampered around like ants on a pile of sugar. The event organizers shouted and pointed fingers and shoved people, trying to regain control. The flow of bodies and the structure of the event started to break down. Nothing worked. The chaos surrounding the president had a life of its own and it demanded to be lived on its own terms.

President Adams stopped to speak to selected people in the crowd, many far too vigorously shaking hands. Air kisses missing the Botox puffed lips of the privileged. The time spent with each calculated before moving on to the next person of note. He steadily made his way toward the more political section of the line, where a little old lady wearing a pillbox hat, white gloves, and a veil awaited.

All the while the show went on, John concentrated on the president and studied his face. He looked as deeply into the eyes of the man as the gathering of people around them would permit. Fortunately, even dressed in his disguise, he was tall enough to be able to see over most people in the area.

When the president was about twenty feet away, he looked directly into John's eyes as if he recognized who he was. The contact lasted for only a millisecond, but it was enough. John saw what he needed to see and more than he hoped for: there was a small cut in the bend of the president's finger.

The president began shaking the hand of each person forming the line leading to the ballroom. He nodded to each one, saying a word or two, as if he knew every one of them intimately. Pictures were taken to immortalize the moment and to provide the person in line with a memento to be mounted on their wall for all to see.

John waited. When President Roger Adams stepped in front of him, their eyes met again. John removed the white glove from his right hand and reached out, taking the president's hand in his. The two shook vigorously as the president leaned forward and lied.

"Good to see you again," he said to John, as if they had met before.

As John released the president's hand, he replied with a single word: "Farewell."

The president hesitated before releasing John's hand and moving on to the next person in line. The expression on his face showing a moment of doubt, as well as acknowledgement of the strange greeting. He continued looking into John's eyes until the next person in line commanded his attention.

John replaced the glove on his right hand and remained standing in the reception line as more dignitaries passed by and entered the ballroom for the next phase of the evening's activities.

Fifteen minutes after shaking Roger Adams' hand, John began easing his way toward the exit. He made certain that he passed within range of two or three security cameras. He wanted to be sure that the image of the woman he portrayed was being captured on film.

He exited via the doors leading to Lexington Avenue. Once outside, he turned to his left and walked north, laying an exit trail that he knew would be traced in the coming days. After walking three blocks, he turned left again, walking west. When he reached Madison Avenue, he turned left once again, walking until he reached 42nd street. There, he made his final turn to the left and walked to Grand Central Station.

In the terminal, he retrieved his duffel bags from the locker. With the large bag over his shoulder and the smaller bag in hand, he walked back out to the street and walked west on 42nd Street. Twenty minutes later, he entered the Port Authority Bus Terminal on 8th Avenue and 40th Street.

He had almost an hour before the next bus to Albany was scheduled for departure. Using that time to his advantage, John took an elevator to the upper parking levels of the terminal building. He walked to the end of the parking level furthest way from the elevators. Sandwiching himself between two vehicles out of sight of cameras and people, he stripped off his female costume and resumed his real identity.

With baseball cap pulled down as low as he could wear it without blinding himself, he returned to the main portion of the terminal and purchased a ticket for the bus he intended to ride toward home. The last thing he had to do before going to the boarding area was to send a coded text message to Bob to meet him at the Albany end of his journey.

Chapter Twenty-Three

It was nearly one in the morning before he tried to slip quietly into the cabin. If Kristin was asleep, he didn't want to wake her up. Not to worry, she was fully awake waiting for him and damn near bowled him over when he entered the cabin, wrapping herself around him and smothering him with kisses. "Oh my God! Oh John! You're safe. Are you okay? Are you hurt?" An uninterrupted stream of questions rushed at him like air off the rear end of an airboat.

"I'm fine, just tired." He saw that the television was on and set to one of the network news channels. "What's going on?" he asked.

"I've been watching to see if anything happened. Nothing has. It's all been very boring. Speech after speech after speech. They announced that Prime Minister DuBois was not feeling well and had retired to his embassy. That's about it. Nothing else but an endless line of fake smiles."

"Good! Emily did her job."

"But he's alive and well. You didn't do anything. What's going on, John?"

"I'm tired, sweetheart. I need some sleep. We can talk in the morning."

"Wait! What? You want me to wait until tomorrow to hear what's going on? Are you crazy? I've been worried sick about you! Pacing the floor for days! And you want me to wait? Are you nuts?"

"Kristin, I love you; I want to lie in bed and hold you and sleep. Nothing is going to change... at least not tonight."

She reluctantly acceded, and they went to bed. Within minutes John was out cold while Kristin sat next to him fidgeting, trying to calm herself. The last time she looked at the clock, it was a little after three.

As usual, the next morning she found John sitting out on the deck drinking his coffee. It was nearly eight o'clock. It was a beautiful day. The temperature was in the mid 60s with a slight breeze coming in from the northwest off the lake. The sun glistened off the crystal clear water.

She came outside carrying a small quilt usually hanging over the back of the couch. She sat in his lap and kissed him warmly. He wrapped her in the quilt, holding her close to ward off the chill in the air.

"Good morning," he said.

"Did you sleep well?"

"Like a baby. Thank you for understanding Kristin. I know—"

Chapter Twenty-Three

She hushed him by placing her index finger to his lips.

"I was being selfish. I'm sorry. Tell me what happened whenever you're ready."

He pointed to the television. The headline story was that the president had cancelled his appearance this morning at an important meeting with the prime minister of Great Britain because of illness. One of the more dramatic newscasters speculated that the president and the prime minister of Canada must have eaten something that resulted in both becoming ill within hours of one another. There were no further details now, nor would there be.

"How about we have breakfast, pack a lunch, and go for a nice long hike?" John suggested.

"I'd really like that. Where are we going?"

"There's a mountain not far from here called Sleeping Beauty. There's a secret place I'd like to show you. It dates back almost a hundred years. Very few people know about it. It's special."

"Sounds wonderful, but what about Bruce?"

"Oh crap, I forgot about him. Where is he?"

"He's at Bob's house. He and his family have been staying there. Bob said it was easier for him to keep a watch on them until you got back. I think it was because Bob's wife wanted to have the kids around for a while. She's been getting a big kick out of them."

"You're probably right. She's a mother first, last, and always. She looks over me the same way. I'll stop over there and have a brief chat with Bruce before we leave. I'm sure he can keep himself busy for one more day. Especially when I tell him that he has nothing to worry about."

By ten o'clock, with a daypack stuffed with food and water on his back, John took Bob's four-wheel-drive ATV and headed off into the woods of the lower Adirondack Mountains. John parked the ATV in an area set aside by the New York State Department of Environmental Conservation for people who wished to ride through the mountains on horseback. Locking the vehicle, he took Kristin by the hand and led her toward the southern base of Sleeping Beauty mountain.

Together they climbed through the thickets of beech and spruce and birch trees. John felt himself being renewed with each step. There was no trail, no path to follow. John bushwhacked through the underbrush, relying only on his instincts and his knowledge of the forest.

The clean mountain air filling his lungs was like a transfusion of life. He'd hiked, hunted, and camped all through this area as a boy and young man. It was only in his adult life that his career in the military, followed by his current job, kept him away from here.

This was where he belonged, his natural habitat. Here, every breath, every step, every wisp of air that brushed across his face, every drop of rain and flake of snow renewed him. He was comfortable in his skin here, confident in his ability to survive and work with Mother Nature on her own terms. He was home!

Kristin followed breathlessly, struggling to keep up, but sensing what was going on within him. She could see the transfusion of energy pumping through him as he became one with the environment. She took his hand whenever he offered it, as he assisted her up and over the more difficult parts of the climb.

When they came to an exposed rock wall overlooking a small plateau, John stopped and sat with his feet dangling over the ledge. He patted the ground, signaling Kristin to sit next to him.

"Look out there." He pointed toward the northwest. "That's Lake George. The Sagamore is not far from there." Well off in the distance, about five miles away, a small area of water was visible through the trees. It sparkled in the sunlight like tinsel on a Christmas tree.

"Oh John," Kristin sighed. It's so beautiful here. So peaceful."

They hadn't seen another human since leaving the parking lot a couple of miles back. There was no noise created by man anywhere within earshot. Just the sounds of the birds chirping and the breeze hissing through the tree tops.

"Down there." John pointed. "See that big white birch tree?"

"Yeah."

"There's a story in these parts that almost a hundred years ago, two hunters shot and wounded a big black bear way back near the Hogtown crossroads. They tailed it, following its tracks and drops of blood for hours. Finally, near dark, after tracking it for miles, they came to a den. All the signs led them to believe the bear was in the den.

They didn't dare enter the small opening, so they decided to smoke it out.

"After a while, the bear came out and they finished the job. It was too late in the day for them to drag it home. They marked that birch tree so they could find it the next day. When they returned, they skinned and butchered the bear and marked where his den was by sticking a cedar log in the ground with their initials and the date carved into it.

"Cedar lasts a long time after it's cut, so after all these years, the marker is still there. Many years ago, one of the old-timers around here led some of my hunting buddies and me to it on the condition that we would never reveal where it was. If we did, sure as shootin,' all kinds of riffraff would come up here and destroy it.

"So we all took an oath that we would keep this location a secret, strictly among the members of our hunt club. You're the first person I've ever brought up here.

"See that big rock on the other side of the clearing? That's another special place for me. I had a very close friend. His name was Scotty. We would come up here to bow hunt every fall. We'd meet on that rock for lunch, and most often we would lean back and take a short nap before we hunted for the rest of the day."

"Where is he now?"

John hesitated for a moment. "Scotty died of leukemia. The doctors did a bone marrow transplant on him, but it didn't work. I haven't hunted this area since he died. Haven't been able to. I've come up here a few times just to sit and be alone. To be with him. To talk to him."

Chapter Twenty-Three

She could hear the crack in his voice, see the emotion on his face. She placed her arm over his shoulders and held him quietly. She could sense what this place and his memories meant to him and how deeply he was affected in this moment on this mountain...his mountain...his and Scotty's mountain.

After a long silence, John shook himself back to the present.

"I'm hungry. Let's eat!"

He unzipped his daypack and they feasted on jerky, hard biscuits, dried figs, and peanut M&M's, all washed down with water from a bottle they had filled at the creek they crossed at the base of the mountain.

After lunch, John leaned back against a large tree and Kristin leaned against him. He draped his arm over her shoulder and held her close. After a while, the wind started to blow, signaling them to begin their walk back to the ATV.

John didn't return the same way they had come. Instead, he led Kristin down the side of the mountain to an improved trail maintained by the forest service. It was wide enough for them to walk side by side, hand in hand. In the silence, there was a feeling between them that something still remained unsaid.

"What is it, John?" she finally asked.

"I'm done, Kristin. I can't return to that life anymore. Not if you are a part of my life, and I very much want you to be. I'm tired of it, and I don't want to be part of the people who are now running this country. There's no honor in it.

"For the first time, I find my mind wandering. My head is filled with all kinds of stuff I've never thought about before. You... me...the two of us together. I can't have both. I can't continue with my life as it was and have you too. The distraction would get me killed, and I would be putting you in a lot of danger.

"It's over. It's got to be over. I just can't do it anymore."

"Good!" she said. "The answer is yes, I am a part of your life, and I want it to stay that way. I don't want to go back there either. If you're done with it, so am I."

They stopped in the middle of the trail and embraced each other. Looking warmly into each other's eyes, they kissed gently, the warm touch of their lips sealing a pact between them. Finally reaching the ATV, they strapped on their helmets and headed back toward the compound and the security of John's little world along the shores of Lake George.

Chapter Twenty-Four

Bruce came running across the lawn from Bob's house as John drove the ATV up to his cabin. He was in a panic.

"He's dead!" he exclaimed.

"Dead? Who's dead?" Kristin asked, startled.

"The president! The president is dead. He died a couple of hours ago. They're reporting that he was assassinated. Poisoned. They're looking for some woman. They think she somehow poisoned him yesterday. It's all over the news. The whole country is on lockdown. Airports, trains, buses, everything. The F.B.I. and every state police force is out looking for this woman. They have her picture plastered everywhere!"

Kristin looked at John. There was no expression of surprise showing on his face. He was going about his business putting the ATV away as if Bruce had not said a word.

"John?" Kristin said.

The Salesman

He simply held his index finger to his lips and continued what he was doing. She and Bruce looked at him, knowing the answer to the question they could not ask. Both knew.

For dinner that night, John built a fire down by the lake and broiled steaks on the open fire. His entire universe was there. He had Bob call Gretchen to join them, along with Bob's wife and Bruce's entire family. He cooked huge steaks and equally big baked potatoes.

Bob's wife supplied the salad, and Gretchen brought the biggest Key lime pie ever baked. The entire group, bound together by actions and events that could not be discussed, enjoyed their meal along with a liberal supply of mild red wine.

John was sure to keep the wine flowing. He knew it would help ease the tension in the minds of those most worried about the day to come. It was only the innocent children who enjoyed themselves simply because of the food and the gathering.

When they had finished eating, John threw more logs on the fire and excused himself while he walked into the cabin. He returned, carrying two duffel bags, one large and one small. He sat next to the fire and unzipped the first bag. He reached in, removed a dress, and tossed it into the fire. Next came a pair of shoes, then a hat—a retro pillbox hat with a grey veil—and a pair of white gloves.

He tossed the two bags into the fire and watched them burn as he picked up a bottle of wine and refilled everyone's glass. Raising his own, he saluted the fire with a single word.

"Farewell!"

They sat silently, mesmerized by the flames. Each knew that this was a turning point in their lives. They also knew that by his actions John had just accepted each of them into his secret life. That he had just placed his life in their hands. He had openly allowed them to witness his confession to the events of the day. Some minutes later, John finally broke the silence.

"Kristin and I will be leaving in a couple of days. Bob, I'd like you to stay here and continue to take care of everything just like you always have. Gretchen, same for you. Bruce, you and your family can move into my cabin while we're gone. Bob will be making long-term living arrangements for you over the next couple of weeks. Once your vacation time is up, you will have some decisions to make.

"Kristin and I will be coming back here when I've taken care of a few things. I'd appreciate it if we all stuck together as a team. I will no longer be traveling like I have in the past. In fact, I plan on spending most of my time right here if you guys will agree to stay on."

Kristin laced her arms around his, resting her face on his shoulder.

Addressing Bob and Gretchen, John said, "You two will continue to receive your salaries and benefits just as you have for all the years you have been here. You might get tired of having me around after a while and decide to kick me out." They all chuckled. "But I'm not sure I would want to be here without you guys.

"Bruce, I don't know what you want to do. I think there will be some big changes in D.C. in the coming months. And I think the coast will be clear for you to return if you want to. It's up to you. All I would ask of you is to forget everything you know about this place, most of all where it's located."

Bruce studied the fire for a moment before answering.

"I think I'll go back to see how things shake out. And I have always been accused of having a very short memory. But I'd like to leave one option open."

"What's that?" John asked.

"If things back there are still as screwed up six months from now, I'd like to be able to come back. There's more peace in this place than I've ever known anywhere."

"That's a deal," John answered. "Now, we've got a few days to kick back and relax. Things need to play themselves out in D.C. and quiet down a bit before any of us move from here."

"But John," Kristin interrupted. "What about the FBI? They're going to be looking for the assassin. Won't they be looking for—?"

"For a big, ugly woman who walks with a cane?"

"Well, yeah."

"Kristin, I've been avoiding police for more years than I want to count in more countries than I can remember. Besides, that ugly woman they're looking for just went up in smoke right here in front of all of us."

Bob spoke up. "In addition, I laid a false trail to cover John. Do you recall when I came and took some of John's clothes from the cabin a couple of days ago?"

She nodded.

Chapter Twenty-Four

"Remember we talked about how John and I have been mistaken for one another over the years? Well, I put that to his advantage. I dressed in his clothes and drove to Syracuse the other day; I made sure I was photographed in a few different places.

"I ran a stop sign right in front of a local cop. When they pulled me over to give me a ticket, I handed them John's identification. So, when he was physically in New York City, he was being photographed and ticketed more than three hundred miles away in Syracuse."

"Like I told you the other day, Kristin," John said. "This is not our first rodeo. Bob has been assisting me for a long time. We have been a team from the very beginning."

They completed the evening with more wine and more relaxed conversation. Gretchen shared a couple of humorous boyhood stories about John and his antics as a local sports hero. Bob also shared a couple of stories that took place during their service together in the Army. Everyone had a good chuckle at John's expense.

As the wine and firewood ran out, so too did the evening, having been sprinkled with a few laughs and jabs at John. He took them as they were meant, in good fun. The breeze off the lake cooled considerably as the night went on. It came time to call it a day. There was a strong sense of regret hovering over the group, regret that their time together was coming to an end.

Gretchen circled the group, giving everyone a farewell hug, lingering a moment longer with John. Bob and his wife said good night and walked to their home, followed closely by Bruce and his little clan. Kristin and John, his arm around her shoulders, walked back to his cabin.

It was agreed that the next few days would be spent relaxing, with some hiking and maybe a canoe trip to one of the islands in Lake George. But no one except Gretchen would leave the confines of the estate.

On the morning of the fifth day following their cookout, Bob drove Bruce, Kristin, and John to the Albany airport, where John rented a car using one of his sets of phony ID's. The three of them then drove south, where Bruce dropped Kristin and John at a self-storage facility on the outskirts of Philadelphia.

After their goodbyes were completed, Bruce was to continue to Washington. He would contact Bob in a few days to make travel arrangements for his family to rejoin him once he was sure all was well.

John and Kristin hooked up the white four-wheel-drive Jeep to the back of their motor home and left the self-storage area behind, taking the same route as they had previously when they left Philadelphia. John's training and discipline, as always, guided him away from roadways with security cameras photographing anything above a vehicle's license plates.

"Where are we going?" Kristin asked, after a few minutes on the road.

"Ottawa," he answered.

Chapter Twenty-Five

Crossing the border this time was no more difficult than it had been less than a week ago. Even with the heightened alert and increased security, a big smile, putting your sunglasses on your forehead, and looking the border agent directly in the eye worked every time. If you followed this routine, John was convinced he could smuggle the entire New York Giants football team across the border and have a tailgate party in the parking lot.

The only difference in this crossing was the place John picked to reenter Canada. He didn't want to raise any flags by crossing too often at the same point and continuing to present themselves as tourists. So this time, instead of the Thousand Islands crossing, he drove north and took the Ogdensburg bridge where he had first attempted to cross into Canada. It seemed like half a lifetime ago.

He had placed a call to the office of Emily Brown to let her know he was coming and wanted to meet with her again. In return, he received a brief text message saying that she would make herself available whenever he arrived in Ottawa.

By design, he and Kristin entered the capital building shortly before five o'clock that afternoon. He informed the security guard that he was expected and would he please advise Ms. Brown that he was in the building. Within a couple of minutes, the two of them were being escorted to the now familiar library.

A few minutes later, Emily, accompanied by Paul Featherstone, joined them. Emily gave John a welcoming hug. The two women also greeted each other warmly.

"I want to thank you for all you did in New York to assure the PM's safety," Paul Featherstone said as he shook John's hand. "I know you put yourself at risk in doing so. We owe you."

Just as Featherstone finished, the door burst open and Prime Minister Peter DuBois unexpectedly entered the room. He extended his right hand, taking John's in a firm grip.

"Good to see you John. I wanted to attend this little get-together to be sure you knew that I very much appreciate what you did. I'm sure it hasn't made your life very simple."

"No sir, it has complicated things a bit. That's for sure."

"And the president's death—?"

"Very regrettable," John replied, his gaze eliminating the need for any further discussion.

Chapter Twenty-Five

"What now?" asked the PM.

"I came here to assure Emily that the threat to you should be over."

It was obvious that there was more to what John wanted to say, but he hesitated, glancing into the face of the three Canadians.

"And—?" Peter DuBois asked again. He picked up on John's hesitation and looked at each person in the room. "Would you rather discuss this privately with Emily?"

John hesitated for another moment. "No sir. It's just very uncommon and unsettling for me to discuss things of this nature with anyone. What I wanted to tell you is that the initial threat is over. I doubt very strongly that there will be any further attempt on your life, especially here in Canada. I think this crazy scheme ended a few days ago. I believe the head of the snake has been cut off."

"You mean with the president's death?"

"Yes."

"There's a 'but' in there somewhere," DuBois sensed.

"Yes, there is. With the president's death, there will be a lot of changes in Washington. I seriously doubt that the vice president had any knowledge of the trumped-up story directed at you."

"But?" the PM asked again.

"But there is assuredly one other person who was involved, and I don't know how reckless he may be."

"I have already increased the personal security guard around the prime minister, as well as his home and family," Featherstone stated strongly.

"I'm sure you have, Mr. Featherstone. And I think that will greatly limit the potential for any further attempts. I just wanted to be sure that you all knew and understood that there is no absolute guarantee in any of this."

"Understood," replied Featherstone.

John continued, addressing Peter DuBois. "I also want you to know that I will attempt to remove any further threat...to either of us."

The conversation continued for another ten minutes before it became awkwardly obvious that it was time to end the meeting. Emily hugged John once again and then turned to Kristin with a much more personal goodbye.

Paul Featherstone shook John's hand and asked that the two men stay in touch should there be any future need. They exchanged contact information. Featherstone and Emily then left the room.

The prime minister shook Kristin's hand and asked, "Would you mind if I had a couple of minutes alone with John?"

"Of course not. I'll wait outside." She looked at John with a worried expression on her face.

Once she was gone, the PM closed the door and invited John to take a seat at the table in the center of the room. He then sat at the opposite side, clasping his hands in front of him, resting his forearms on the table.

Chapter Twenty-Five

"I wanted to have a moment to thank you privately for what you did. I think I know enough about the world you operate in to know that you have potentially put yourself in grave danger. Should you ever find it necessary, I can and will take immediate steps to grant you Canadian citizenship and have all the necessary documents prepared for you to take up residence in Canada. We can assist you in... being absorbed into our society."

John thought for a moment before answering. "Thank you, Mr. Prime Minister. I'll know in a few days if I will need to take you up on that offer. I greatly appreciate what you are offering."

"I presume that the lovely Ms. Blake would also need the same assistance?"

"Should I need to take you up on your offer, yes sir, she would also need the same extended to her."

"Consider it done."

John stood, assuming that their meeting was over. The prime minister, however, didn't rise to his feet.

"One more thing," he said as John resumed his seat. "Is there any way that you, as a man having certain professional skills, can explain to me how a little old lady, in possession of documents showing her to be a member of the Canadian delegation I might add, using a cane to assist her walking, was somehow able to disappear into thin air? Might she have been responsible for the death of the president of the most powerful nation on earth? Just how might such a person have carried out such a mission?"

"Have you watched any of the security films?" John asked.

"Hours of them!" DuBois replied.

"And?" John asked.

"We saw nothing. You— The little old woman never raised her hand, never raised her cane, never revealed a weapon of any kind. She simply shook hands with the president and the next day, he's dead and she's gone."

"Look again."

"John, I'm not a stupid man, but neither I nor any of my top security people were able to pick up a thing. We all know that this little old woman probably saved my life or at the very least, removed a big threat. So, please, with my assurance that her secret will never leave this room."

"The hand."

"The hand?"

"Yes. The right hand to be exact. Between my—the old woman's—hand and the white glove. Look closely. You might detect a slightly shiny glaze. Under the glove on the right hand is a very thin protective layer of Teflon. It creates a barrier. Then, before the glove is put on, a few drops of an extremely deadly poison found in the Amazon jungles of Brazil. Our lady friend just happened to visit there in recent months. Just a few drops are required.

"The poison will not penetrate the Teflon. But, when it encounters naked skin, let's say as in a very firm and prolonged hand shake, it is absorbed into the recipient's body. It then slowly circulates through the blood stream, paralyzing the heart muscle resulting in a very slow, unstoppable death.

"Usually takes twelve to sixteen hours…or so I've been told. I've also been told by someone I know, that the Amazon natives sometimes use this poison to do away with a tribal enemy.

"The person to whom the poison has been administered remains fully conscious and aware of what's going on around them, but can't communicate. Therefore, the person dying knows that he is dying and can't do a damn thing about it… except die.

"After the handshake, the white glove is replaced to protect the person wearing it and anyone else…she…may happen to touch. Both the Teflon skin and the glove are then peeled off, sort of like a glove within a glove. The gloved left hand prevents contamination and the Teflon is discarded, let's say, in a public toilet in the world's largest bus terminal and simply disappears forever into the vast sewage-treatment facilities of New York City.

The two men looked at each other, each taking the measure of the other, each accepting the other as an equal.

"And the little old woman?" the prime minister asked.

"I believe she too has probably disappeared. If not permanently, she certainly won't be attending any more affairs as a Canadian diplomat.

The prime minister broke the silence. "Well," he said, "Thank you for sharing your…expertise with me. I'll be sure to be more careful around little old ladies wearing white gloves."

"Only if they happen to have recently traveled to the Amazon jungle," John replied as he stood to take the PM's hand. Dubois looked down and with a smile on his face, cautiously took John's hand, shaking it firmly.

They left the small room, maybe not as friends, but more like two men having stood side by side in combat, one surviving as the result of the bravery of the other. There was now an invisible bond forever linking the two of them in a way only men having a similar experience would know and understand.

An hour later, with the white Jeep reattached to the rear bumper of the motor home, John and Kristin began the drive back to the United States. He drove the QEW 401 toward Toronto, ultimately crossing back into the U.S. via the Rainbow Bridge at Niagara Falls, a heavily-used tourist crossing. He wanted to get lost in the multinational mix of people driving and walking across the bridge.

He rented a space in a nearby RV park, which they could use as home base while they spent two quiet days together enjoying the sights. In the morning, they toured Niagara Falls, John checking to see if they were being followed by anyone from either side of the border. He led Kristin in and out of front and rear doors of hotels and eateries until he was confident that they were alone and safe. Old habits die hard.

John grew more and more confident that he was out of immediate danger. Knowing Bruce had erased his personnel file from the agency's records also made him feel that he had a future to look forward to.

Chapter Twenty-Five

But he wasn't totally confident…yet. It would be awhile before he stopped looking over his shoulder to see, as a famous ballplayer once said, "if anyone was gaining on him."

The second morning, they walked along the top of the American Falls and took the mandatory excursion on the Maid of the Mist to the base of the Horseshoe Falls, riding up the space needle on the Canadian side. The day ended with another great dinner together. The following morning, it was time to once again, point the motor home east and begin the trek across New York State.

John made his way to U.S. 20, the old Boston Post Road, to avoid the camera-laden New York State Thruway. They drove through the tiny towns scattered throughout the lush dairy country of western New York. They drove across the northern end of the Finger Lakes, passing through the town of Skaneateles, a place whose name even the locals had a difficult time spelling correctly.

Their next night was spent in a campground not too far north of Cooperstown, where the baseball hall of fame is located. In the morning, John drove north on I-88, taking the last exit before the Thruway. He picked his way around Schenectady, through Ballston Spa, and Saratoga Springs, re-entering I-87 for the final short drive north to Lake George and home. Their warm and secure cabin awaited them.

Once inside and settled, John called Bob and asked him to join them. When he arrived at the cabin, the three of them sat in the den, each holding a comforting mug of the hot chocolate Kristin had whipped up while waiting for Bob.

After a few minutes of small talk about nothing, John got down to the real purpose of their gathering.

"There are a few things we need to get done," he said to Bob. "I want you to know that I intend to retire from my current...um...occupation. But first, there is one more thing I should take care of. Once I've taken care of this final detail, I will be here in the compound a lot more than I have been in recent years. Because of that, you need to make a list of what that would mean to you, your workload and duties, a list of things you would need to secure the grounds. Money is not an object. Do it and do it right!"

"Do you see any change in my long-term employment status?" Bob asked.

"None!" John answered. "It's me who will have to come up with something to do. You can work for me for the rest of your life, and I sincerely hope that you do. I can assure you, after the last assignment, I have plenty of money to survive the rest of our lives. You and Gretchen will always be taken care of for as long as you wish to stay."

"Okay. And thank you. My wife will be very happy to hear that. She's felt a little unsettled lately."

"One thing you need to take into consideration," John continued. "I think there will be two of us. I want Kristin to stay here and make this her home, too."

Kristin looked across the room at John with the face of a woman who had just been handed the keys to the happiness locker. She tried to recapture her composure by first closing her mouth. She damn near spilled the mug of hot chocolate into her lap.

"Did you just propose to me? Is that your smooth way of asking me to marry you?" she finally squeezed through her chocolate-scorched lips.

"Well… yeah!" John fumbled.

"You slick, romantic devil!" Bob said with a big grin on his face. "I think I'd better step outside and finish what I was doing."

"No, hold on!" John said.

"No, I think the lady has something she might want to say. I'll make my list and we'll talk later," Bob said as he headed for the door.

"Wait!" John pleaded, but Bob waved him off as he walked out the door.

Kristin walked across the room and stood in front of John. She put her hands on her hips and looked down at him.

"On your knees, big boy!" Once John had lowered himself to the floor, she continued. "Now, ask me like I was the love of your life and not some damned old drinking buddy here for Monday night football."

Chapter Twenty-Six

John arrived in Washington, D.C. aboard an Amtrak train from Philadelphia, where he had returned the motor home to the storage facility. He checked into a room in the Marriott on 14th street. From there, he made a series of calls using half a dozen burner phones.

A meeting was arranged with Bruce. They were to meet at the Vietnam Memorial later that afternoon. On the way to the meeting, he took a taxi to the office of a local moving and storage company. He arranged for them to enter Kristin's apartment to pack up everything in it and deliver the load to a certain self-storage facility on the outskirts of Philadelphia. He left them with the key to her apartment, as well as the key to a currently empty storage unit. Finally, he left them with a considerable amount of cash to pay for their services, as well as their complete discretion.

At the agreed time, he stood next to Bruce at the Vietnam Wall. Neither acknowledged the presence of the other. Their conversation was brief and to the point. Bruce supplied John with certain information he had asked for when they talked on the phone. Then John delivered a message of his own.

"Bruce, you know where to find me. You're the only person alive who knows where I live. If I didn't trust you, you'd be dead. I told you before, but let me repeat it once again. You want out of this rat race, you have a place to go. You and your family. You can contact me through Bob just as you did the first time."

When he was done talking, he handed Bruce an envelope containing Kristin's formal resignation from her government position. Also included was the address of a UPS store in Shallotte, North Carolina, where her mail, including her final paycheck, was to be sent. Then he simply walked away.

It was mid-October. Football season was in full swing. William Baxter, the former White House Chief of Staff who had ordered Bruce to arrange the assassination of the prime minister of Canada, was an avid Washington Redskins fan and a season ticket holder. This Sunday found the Skins hosting their division rival, the New York Giants.

Although Baxter was now unemployed because of the death of his close friend, the president, and the massive changes made in the administration by the new president, he was in no way lacking any of the comforts of life. He was a wealthy man and could well afford the box seats that he currently shared with three of his closest friends.

The game was in the middle of the third quarter, Giants leading 27 to 13 and driving. The ball was on the Redskins' 37-yard line, and the crowd was in a near panic as the Redskins were about to go down yet another score.

Another 3 or 7 points didn't much matter at this late stage of the game.

A man carrying a tray containing four beers walked by the Baxter box seat. He stumbled, accidentally spilling a cup of cold brew on Baxter's leg. Once the mandated apology was completed, the man carrying the beer disappeared into the crowd.

The spill, however, demanded that Baxter retreat to the men's room to clean himself up a bit. He angrily excused himself and headed toward the closest men's room.

Ten minutes later, emerging from the men's room, he immediately bumped into a rather large man who suddenly stepped into his path. Baxter was knocked to the ground. The second man did not even stop to apologize, he just walked directly to an exit and departed the stadium.

As Baxter attempted to regain his footing, a rather tall older woman leaning on a cane removed her white glove from her right hand and extended it to the once-powerful White House Chief of Staff. He took her hand and gripped it tightly, accepting the assist to regain his footing.

Back on his feet, Baxter brushed himself off and turned to thank the woman who was kind enough to offer him her assistance. He looked her in the eye, feeling that he had somewhere seen her face before.

"Thank you," he said.

"You're very welcome," she answered. "Have a great day. Farewell!"

Chapter Twenty-Six

The little old lady patted the back of his hand and turned away, replacing her glove as she walked beneath the sign that said 'EXIT,' disappearing into the throng of fans, never to be seen again.

Chapter Twenty-Seven

Life in the mountains is a never-ending cycle of seasons. Spring followed by summer followed by fall followed by winter, only to begin again. One could take the completion of each as an ending. Kristin preferred to take each as the beginning of yet another new season.

A year had somehow slipped by. Four seasons had come and gone. She entered each with the delight of a child. Each brand new to her, presenting exciting challenges and experiences.

She had never seen the brilliant display of colors the mountains presented in the fall. The leaves changed from what seemed to be a million shades of green to an equal number of different reds, browns, yellows, and oranges. She hiked through the forest, climbed the mountains, waded across the streams, losing herself in the vastness and peace of her new surroundings.

The winter cold brought ice and snow, changing the lake and the surrounding hills into a crystal wonderland.

Chapter Twenty-Seven

She learned to cross-county ski, to drive a snowmobile, to icefish. She found it exciting to challenge the elements and walk across frozen Lake George in temperatures well below zero. She learned the language of the ice as it moaned and groaned, shifting from the wind and the ever-changing temperatures.

Spring—glorious spring with the beauty and scent of new growth and mountain wildflowers. All around her she witnessed the rebirth of nature.

Summer brought boating and fishing and more hiking and cool nights in the arms of her new husband.

And John. John was there with her, leading the way, keeping his promises. Taking her everywhere. Showing her everything. Teaching her all about his world, their new world. They had grown together. Their love had magnified and become greater with each passing day. They shared everything, making up for all the years spent without one another.

John learned to forget. He learned to accept his new life, to stop looking over his shoulder. His life had changed. And so had everything that had once controlled and dictated his every breath.

With the help of Bruce, his past life had been obliterated. Wiped clean as if it had never existed. The hunt for the president's assassin continued. The FBI was at a loss. They could find no trail leading them to the woman thought to be the killer. The Canadian government cooperated fully, but denied knowing who the woman was or having ever issued diplomatic documents to anyone matching her description. The hunt cooled with speculation that the assassin had fled the country.

The Salesman

In a private compound tucked in along the shores of Lake George, everyone continued to refer to one of the residents as John. It wasn't his real name. But it was easier to just be John. Too much would be needed to explain otherwise. It was time to keep life simple. So John it was. And John it would remain.

However, to all that was the old John, to all that the old John had been, this John bade farewell.

About the Author

Richard Totino was raised on an apple farm in the town of Marlboro in the mid-Hudson Valley of New York. Although he has traveled extensively, he still considers himself to be a small-town boy with small-town values. After his enlistment in the U.S. Army, he returned to college to complete his graduate degrees at the ripe old age of 34. His work in international sales and marketing provided him with an insight into many cultures and customs beyond our borders, and his extensive travel in the U.S. taught him that people everywhere are as open and friendly as you give them the opportunity to be. He likes to tell people, "I have slept in 49 states," which leads his wife to describe him as George Washington, who seems to have slept everywhere.

Dick and his wife, Sharon, now reside in North Carolina, where they soak up the sunshine and sea breezes. Their combined family includes eight children and five grandchildren, providing them with plenty to do and all the related challenges that go with keeping up with a large family.

An avid hunter and outdoorsman, Dick's personal experiences enhance his writing. He refers to fall as "scrapbooking season," because that's when he leaves Sharon at home to occupy herself with her crafts while he escapes to the wilderness of North Carolina and the Adirondack Mountains of New York. He has been active in the Knights of Columbus, the Elks, Disabled American Veterans, the American Legion and as crew boss with Lower Adirondack Search and Rescue (LASAR), participating in numerous search and rescue efforts throughout the region.